RATNA TRANSLATION SERIES

ECHOES OF THE VEENA

AND OTHER STORIES

R. CHUDAMANI

I0557252

TRANSLATED FROM TAMIL BY

PRABHA SRIDEVAN

RATNA BOOKS

Published by **RATNA BOOKS**
An imprint of Ratna Sagar P. Ltd.
Virat Bhavan, Mukherjee Nagar Commercial Complex
Delhi 110009, India
www.ratnabooks.in

To
Brian Harris,
with gratitude, for sharing
his passion for translation
and
Savitri Paatti,
with gratitude, for passing on
her genes of translation

Contents

one

Timepass

THE SUNLIGHT HIT VANJI'S EYES fiercely when she came out from the darkness of her home. Home was a small hole-like room. There were ten such rooms, known as 'portions', each of which was a 'home'. She closed her eyes and opened them again, but her eyes still smarted with the brightness.

The heat kept rising sharply. She had finished her daily chores at home and had eaten the food that her mother had cooked before she left for work, after feeding her little brother. The clothes had been washed and hung to dry. This was the hour of languor, not yet noon. The whole day was before her; her mother would return only at seven.

She was restless, eager to do something.

Doesn't that light blue sky look like plain blue paper, spread out there within reach? It would be lovely if she could just run up and touch it. She would have done something then.

Fed up, she turned to look inside the house. Just outside the door of their 'portion' the child was playing happily with a broken plastic lid. This Solai chap was no bother if he was fed regularly. Sometimes she wished he had been a troublesome child. Minding and looking after him would then have been a full-time job.

Her mother had discontinued her studies so that she could look after her little brother…The resentment bubbled within her.

Why didn't her grade V teacher say: 'I won't take class without S. Vanjikkodi'?

Suddenly, the child smiled at her sweetly. Vanji made faces at him. Soon the child would recognize her face more easily than her mother's. The thought annoyed her.

She came in. The child dropped the plastic lid, and dragging the diaper cloth that was trailing from the loin-thread into which it was tucked, crawled towards her. When she sat down, he buried himself in her lap.

He was one year old and still did not know how to walk. Wretched brat, why was he born? Why couldn't he have died too, like the other three babies born after her?

She bent down towards her little brother. Her bubbling anger gave way to a gush of affection when she saw the child pressing his cheek on her lap, knowing he was safe with her. She patted him.

'Solai, are you sleeping?'

Solai was not sleeping. He turned his face and struggled

to sit up when she patted him. When he pressed forward to sit up, his teeth bit into her lap and she screamed in pain.

'Biting me, you wretch? You behave like a dog…I'm staying at home and not going to school because of you and you bite me? You cursed one! You dirty shit!'

She whacked him hard on his back. She lifted her cheap cotton skirt to inspect her thigh. Though it really did not hurt, she felt like crying when she saw two tiny teeth marks. Thoughts of her mother, her school, the father who had died and her brother, who had not, fused into a rage which got transformed into blows on his back.

'Will you bite me again? Will you?'

The child wailed loudly, drawing the attention of the women in the other 'portions'.

'Vanji, why are you thrashing him? Ay-yay-yo, how can you be so cruel?'

'Do you know what this devil did? He bit me!'

'As if he did it on purpose…He is just a baby, doesn't know what he is doing. He will feel like chewing things at this age; it's for us to be careful. You can't hit him like a demon because of this. Just wait, we will tell your mother.'

'Get out, all of you. How is it your concern what I do to my brother? Do you take care of him? Why didn't you tell my mother that you will take care of him so that I could go to school? Easy for you to now come and lecture me. Just go away.'

'My! What impertinence at thirteen. Go to hell!' They went away.

3

Vanji's temper had subsided. She looked at her brother, who was still crying, his cheeks shining with tears.

'Mmm…stop it…enough. Won't you stop? Come here.'

She pulled him to her and wiped the tears off his face, and she realized she was weeping too. She did not know why. She wiped her eyes too.

'What are you going to do now? Sleep?'

Solai shook his head, as if to say 'no'. He crawled and moved away from her, afraid that she might force him down to sleep.

'What is this long tail behind you? Little monkey!'

She tied the cloth properly.

'Why are you crawling even now? Stand up and walk. I'm telling you, stand up.'

She picked him up and made him stand. She peeled away the tiny hands stuck to her shoulders and stood him up so that her shoulders were out of his reach. Whimpering with fear, the child tottered for a moment and fell with a thud and started crying.

'Che che, you must not cry. If you act like this, when will you ever stand up and walk? Good boy, Solai. Come, grip the wall…Walk.'

Vanji made him stand next to the wall.

'Mmm, hold the wall, now walk.'

The child clung to her legs, covered in a skirt, and refused to walk. She pulled his hands and made him grip the wall.

'Walk, you idiot.'

Step by step, at first a bit afraid and then a bit confident, he made progress holding on to the wall. He smiled as if elated by the triumph. When he reached the end of the wall, he carefully slid to the floor and sat down.

'Mmm…do it again.'

After he had done this five or six times, Vanji said, 'Now let's see if you can do it without any support,' and made him stand in the centre of the room. The child tried to take a step forward, but fell down. He started to cry again.

'Don't yell, don't yell. The stupid thing doesn't know how to walk, but can cry loudly.'

The wailing did not cease. Vanji took a bunch of flat plastic spoons from a tin in the corner and threw it in front of her brother.

Whenever the people who lived in one of the upstairs 'portions' had ice cream, they washed the ice cream spoons. They had strung together a dozen of them and given it to Solai to play with. It looked attractive, as the spoons were of different colours. Since they made a noise when one shook them, they served as a rattle too. This was Solai's favourite toy.

As soon as Vanji brought it to him, he stopped crying and crawled towards it. He then looked at her happily and lisped something, splattering saliva all over.

'Kkk kaaya viviyuchchattu…'

Wretch, can't say any word except Amma. But it seemed like he now said 'Kkaa' more often. This pleased her a lot.

'Do you know I stay at home only because of you? If you don't say "Akka" – elder sister – properly in the next ten days…I'll kill you. Just wait.'

The child paid her no heed. He was happily playing with his rattle.

Vanji looked at the clock on the stand.

This was one of the few things that her father had purchased.

She would often imagine that the tick-tock of the clock was his heartbeat, that he had never died of fever, that he was still working as an attendant in an office, that her mother did not go to work but stayed at home and above all, that she was skipping along and going to school with her two plaits swinging and her books and pencils in her hand.

She was lost in her thoughts for a while. Then she shook her head and came back to reality. She looked at the clock. It was one.

'Will you sleep at least now?'

Solai did not turn around. Vanji went to the kitchen and had a glass of water.

'Solai, shall I play with you? Shall we play "muttu muttu"?'

She came close to her brother to knock her head against his in what was the muttu muttu game. He humphed and pulled his head away.

'Hmm. It is for this child that they have stopped my schooling.'

Vanji fumed. She got up to sweep the house, repeating a chore she had already done once in the morning. She was startled when she lifted her head. The child had curled up with his toy and gone to sleep.

Oh shit! So he won't even let me do the job of putting him to sleep... Such a bore.

She threw the broom in exasperation and thumped him on the back. The child woke up with a start and began to cry.

'Fool, shut up now. You sat mutely when I kept asking if you would go to sleep. And then if you fall asleep on your own, why should I be here to look after you? Come here and lie down properly on the mat. You bum.'

She stood him up and dragged him by his hand as he wept and wailed. She spread an old sheet on the mat and put him on it. He cried some more.

'I'll kill you if you don't stop now.'

She pressed his face on the mat and patted him. He struggled and howled, turning his head this way and that. Vanji slapped him hard again.

'Monster...howling like this.'

She closed his eyes with one hand and patted him on the back with the other. The crying turned into sobs.

Suddenly, he lifted his head and moved towards her and put his head on her lap. He whimpered as if pleading with her. Vanji took one look at the tear-stained face. She lifted her brother and hugged him. She wiped his eyes, kissed him on his cheek and put him on her lap. He went to sleep with a smile.

She laid him properly on the mat and resumed sweeping the house for the second time. She realized she had nothing else to do...unless she swept the house for the third time.

Shall I go and sit outside? But no one will be on the streets at this time of the afternoon. She thought of her friends with whom she had studied, and who were still studying in school. She envied them and cried silently. She wiped her face and tried to sleep, lying next to the child. The child kicked her as he rolled over in his sleep. Cursing him, she tapped him on his foot. She could not sleep.

She went upstairs and asked the owner's wife for a Tamil weekly magazine. She came down and putting a pillow against the wall, stretched out with the magazine.

She read the jokes first. Her eyes got riveted to the illustrations accompanying the stories. Remembering that her mother had told her not to look at them, she quickly turned those pages over and read only the snippets of information. But her hand went to those pages on its own. She kept staring at them for a while.

Men…and women…could there be such poses?…Yuck… bad…she mustn't see them. Why do these women wear their saris this way? If her half-sari moved off her shoulder even a bit, her mother would bark at her to cover herself properly! Che…che…filthy…She mustn't see them.

She looked at the pictures involuntarily and became conscious of her body. For a moment, she looked down at herself. Overcome by inhibition, she covered herself properly with the half-sari. But she could not tear her eyes away from those pictures. Her mind and body felt an unfamiliar arousal. Smut, smut…why are these wretched things published?

Determined not to look at those pictures, she began to read a story. What she had seen in the images was described in words in the stories. She could not understand it fully, but she read on with interest. When she came across an illustration, she covered it with her left hand. As she continued to read, she was aware that there was a picture she could see merely by lifting her hand.

She woke up with a start. The magazine had fallen beside her. It was three. The child was making soft, whimpering sounds. Had she gone to sleep while reading?

Thank goodness! It was three and there was some work to be done. She got up briskly and went upstairs to return the magazine.

Solai was sitting up.

'Little one, got up, is it? Will you have milk?'

As she came up to him, asking him this affectionately, she found that the child had wet the mat and the cloth.

'Idiot! How many times have I told you not to piss on the mat?'

Even as she shouted angrily, she remembered that it was she who had been at fault for not taking him to the toilet before he had gone to sleep. She stopped shouting.

She made the boy stand up with his hands on her shoulders. She removed the wet clothes, wiped the mat and threw the clothes into a corner. She took him to the toilet, made him stand up and tied a dry napkin, like a loin cloth. She carried the mat and spread it in the backyard to dry. Her mother would yell if she saw it was wet.

She went to the kitchen and heated the watery milk

she had saved from the morning. She poured it into an aluminium cup and got the child to drink it. She could have coffee only after she got fresh milk at four. They bought a quarter litre of milk in the morning and boiled it, adding some water. After she and her mother had coffee, and her brother his milk, there would be just enough for the child to drink in the afternoon.

'Ah good, all done. Now shall we practise walking?'

The child did not cooperate at all. Even though she made him stand next to the wall, he pulled himself away from her and sat down to play with his rattle, happily.

'Stupid kid, when will you learn to walk and to talk?'

'Chchcaatttattathuppiykkaa...'

'Idiot, look at you, you ass.'

She drew Ludo-like squares on the floor with chalk and started playing with herself by tossing the coins.

'Throw the one...Five, five come on five, cut the enemy!... That's twelve. So I have to play again.'

The great advantage of this was that whichever coin won, she was the victor.

Suddenly, the child, his interest aroused by what she was doing, crawled up swiftly and with one swipe at the white squares, pushed all the coins away.

'Demon, devil, pig, wish you were dead.' Before she could hit him, the child moved away and sat with the plastic spoons. He rejoiced at the noise of the spoons banging on the floor.

Vanji cursed him with an unprintable expletive. Then she picked up the coins to play again. But stung with irritation,

R. CHUDAMANI (1931–2010) was a prolific writer in Tamil and English. Sitting in her room, from where she could see a Nagalinga tree, she wrote with empathy about a wide spectrum of issues concerning women, children and men. Though keeping a low profile, she made a niche for herself in the Tamil literary world through her sensitive portrayal of people around her. She won several literary awards, such as the Kalaimagal Silver Jubilee Award, the Ananda Vikatan Prize, the Ilakkia Chintanai (short story of the month) Award, the Bombay Tamil Sangam Silver Jubilee Prize and the State Government Award. She has 32 volumes of fiction to her credit. These include novels, plays and short story collections. She bequeathed all her property to three charities.

Based on her seven short stories (including three from this collection), the Madras Players in 2016 staged a play titled *Chudamani*. The continued success and the overwhelming response to this play from young and old is testimony to her universal appeal.

PRABHA SRIDEVAN is a former judge of the Madras High Court (2000–2010) and the former chairperson of the Intellectual Property Appellate Board (2011–2013). Her judgments have dealt, among other things, with the right to freedom of speech, protection of water bodies, protection of heritage buildings, rights of the oppressed classes, rights of persons with disabilities, right to information, right to education, rights of children, gender equality, mental health, the economic worth of a homemaker's work, compulsory licensing of a cancer drug, and challenge by Novartis to India's Patent Act. She writes regularly in English and Tamil on issues of law and life. *Seeing in the Dark* (OUP, 2015), a collection of short stories by Chudamani, was her first work of translation. This is her second.

This collection of eighteen stories in English translation is vintage Chudamani. The stories explore a variety of themes, such as the psychological landscape of a girl who had to stop going to school, of the insecurity of a mother who sucks the life out of her child, of a deserted woman who stands tall with her self-respect intact, of the loneliness of a forgotten actor of yester-years. Two stories tell the tales of two exceptional musicians (both dead) and their wives; but the likeness ends there. Two stories speak of two fathers and their daughters; but the similarity ends there. In the midst of simple, straightforward narration, the master storyteller makes a sharp, ironic comment on social barriers and taboos.

Chudamani understood children, she understood persons with disabilities; she understood men too. But many of her stories centre around the woman with her anxieties in the role of a wife, sister or mother. She tells us: this is how She is, She feels, and She lives and struggles. Chudamani does not judge; nor does she say that the woman is perfect.

she made faces at her brother's back, left the coins in a pile and went out.

She sat on the porch steps and watched the passersby in the street. The shit that lay near the gutter, thanks to the kids, made her feel sick. She went in.

It was four. Vanji took a vessel and some coins, carried her brother, along with his rattle, on her hip, locked the main door of her portion and walked to Gopal Milk Depot two streets away. Every day when she saw the cows and the calves and all the activity there, she wished that even if she did not go to school, she should at least work at some place like this.

Konar poured a quarter litre of milk into her vessel and generously added a bit more, as usual, saying this was for little Solai. Vanji smiled by way of thanking him and returned after giving him the change.

She came home, boiled the milk and made herself some coffee. She cooked some rice and some eggplant. There was some leftover food that her mother had made in the morning – that would be enough. She pulled off the washed clothes drying on the line and folded them. She wiped her brother's face and made him wear a new shirt. She combed her hair. She straightened the clothes she was wearing. Her half-saris were made of the fairly intact parts of her mother's torn saris.

'Let me earn a little, I will get a new half-sari for you, my dear Vanjikkodi.' In those special moments of affection, her mother would call her by her full name.

She took the rice off the stove. She washed her face,

11

sprinkled some powder on herself and stood facing the street with the child at her hip. She stood there watching for a while. It was past five and the narrow street was busy with cycles, cycle-rickshaws and pedestrians.

She could see two women filling their pots with water from the street tap near the Pillayar temple. Soon she grew tired of this too.

The evening chores were done. Her mother would be home to feed the child and do the rest of the work. Vanji need not do anything else. Why couldn't she go out now?

The last few days, she had been going to the Gangadhareswarar temple in the evening. She didn't feel like going there now.

How about visiting a friend?

Her former classmates were no longer that friendly. Even those willing to play with her objected to her bringing the child along. Where could she leave this wretched kid? If there had been a place where one could leave him, she need not have stopped going to school. He was no trouble at all. He remained in the same place, playing with his toys. But her friends did not allow her to bring him along.

The other tenants were not willing to take care of him.

'How can we take responsibility for someone else's child? If he falls by chance, it is we who will be blamed,' they mumbled and moved away.

It may be a good idea to go to the park today.

She locked the house and stepped out, carrying the child.

The sun had ripened into a nice golden yellow by the time she reached the Nehru Park. Vanji deeply inhaled the sweetness of the breeze blowing over her.

There were not many people in the park. She sat on a cement bench with her brother next to her. The child stood up holding the back of the bench and walked back and forth, amusing himself. She tried to pass the time, looking at the trees, the flowers and the green grass.

He came and sat down on the bench opposite her. He was wearing tight pants, had a thin moustache and not very long hair...maybe twenty-six or twenty-seven. He was eating Dasaprakash ice cream with a plastic spoon.

At first, Vanji did not see him. He was staring at her, she noticed. She felt a little uneasy and looked away. She looked back at him every now and then to see if his eyes were still on her. Whenever she did so, he was looking at her. He did not turn away when she looked at him. On the contrary, when she had looked at him like that four or five times, he gave her a smile. Vanji was not sure if she should smile back. Oddly, she was a bit scared. She firmly turned her head away.

But he did not stop staring at her. Adolescence was struggling to free itself from her child's body – this had a special charm. He did not stop staring at her.

When she looked at him surreptitiously, he gave her a wide smile.

'The ice cream is good. Want one?'

She did not expect that he would talk to her and was

startled. She did not reply.

Wasn't it wrong to talk to strangers?

'Why don't you answer? Don't you want ice cream? The ice cream man has not gone too far. I'll call him and buy one for you.'

She still did not say a word. Her hands felt cold. Nothing to be scared about in his smile or words. Didn't he sound friendly?

'Tell me, my child. What am I to do if you don't answer? Want an ice cream? Don't be scared. Tell me.'

'No.' A quavering low voice.

'Why? Don't you like ice cream? Afraid of a sore throat?'

'I don't want anything. But if you don't mind, give me the spoon after you are done with it,' she said with some hesitation.

'Just the spoon? What will you do with it?'

'He likes it. This is his rattle.' She showed him the bunch of spoons.

'Smart idea! I'll surely give it to you…Is he your brother?'

'Yes.'

'Are there other brothers and sisters at home?'

'No, no. Only him…There were others, but they died.' She seemed to feel more confident.

'Oh! All of them died? Sorry. Where is your father?'

'He is dead too.'

'Whaaat? He too? Amma? Is at least she alive or…?' he asked with a laugh. She chuckled involuntarily.

'Oh yes! She is a helper in a nursing home in Adyar. My

father's employer gave her his job out of compassion. If she takes the bus to work at seven in the morning, she will return only at seven in the evening.'

'And what do you do? Do you go to school?'

'I used to, but after Appa died and Amma started to work, I had to stop going to school to look after this boy and home,' she said with a little sadness but concluded in a happy tone. 'I take good care of him.'

'Bravo! That's a good girl. What's your name?'

'S. Vanjikkodi. My brother is S. Solai. Aren't you Solai, little one?'

'Chheeyyvooyyaa.'

'Can't he speak?'

'Not yet. But he makes noises like this…he is very fond of me.'

'Is that so? Very good.' The way he kept looking at her made her feel uncomfortable and at the same time, strangely excited. Those pictures in that magazine flashed across her mind.

'Where is your house, Vanjikkodi?'

She told him her address on Velaalar Street.

'No one calls me Vanjikkodi, just Vanji.'

'Do you come here every day, Vanji?'

'No, no. Not every day, just once in a way. If I am too bored, I come here and sit for some time. All because of this brat…I cannot go to school, nor play with my friends.'

She could speak naturally now – no fear or hesitation.

'That's okay. Come here every day and I will too. We can

15

chat. I will tell you stories and all that is happening in the city.'

'Truly?'

'Yes.'

'May I bring this one along? I can't leave him alone at home. He is very well-behaved. If we give him a toy, he will keep playing in the same spot. He will not trouble us.'

'Certainly. I like him very much too. Hey Solai, I will wash this spoon and bring it tomorrow, little fellow. Vanji, come to the park from now on, okay?'

'I will.' Her eyes glowed.

He stared at her. He too was bored. He had finished his studies long ago. He had not found a job. He had participated in the agitation demanding employment, burnt buses. He had joined various political parties, shouted slogans. When foreign films were shown, he bought tickets for four rupees, sold them for twenty. Such activities entertained him and kept him occupied in his jobless state. Looking at this girl, it occurred to him that she might be a source of entertainment for him.

'Start coming from tomorrow, Vanji, okay? I will come too. If you come here, then we can also go to other places. I will take you…and Solai too. See you tomorrow?'

'Sure.'

'At what time?'

If she finished cooking at four, she could leave as soon as she had her coffee. Then it would be all right if she returned home before Amma came back…

'By four-thirty.'
'Come definitely.'
'Oh yes.'

When she returned home carrying Solai after saying 'ta-ta'
to that man, her heart was bubbling with joy. What a relief!
From now on she wouldn't have to struggle with boredom.
The morning would go by in anticipation of the evening and
the preparation for it. Time would fly in the park with this
man…Park…and he had also promised to take her to other
places…

From tomorrow, time would pass happily for Vanji.

Amma didn't know…

Poor Amma.

two

He Came as a Guest

NATESAN SAID THAT THE GUESTS would come in the evening, after four. But Sugandhi was ready by three.

Natesan looked at his wife keenly. She was more radiant than the golden border that made a shining contrast between her moss green sari and blouse. Her ornaments were usually stored away in the jewel box, but today, the delicate gold necklace gleamed around her neck next to the tali, a sign that she was married.

Had she dressed especially for the guests? Had she missed socializing so much? Visits to the ladies' club four evenings a week were her only social outings. In this forest area, visitors were rare.

Engineers who work in dense forests should not get married, at his age and to a beautiful woman like her.

The rain had stopped after two days. The gentle warmth of the sun blended with the coolness from the trees.

'I pray that it does not rain today.' Sugandhi was worried that the rain might drive away the guests. She came and stood near him. 'How do I look?'

Natesan could not reply. Did her beauty depend on what she wore? Did the sun's rays need to be gilded?

'You don't like this?'

The wide, smiling eyes and lips drooped in a moment. Natesan felt as if he had slapped a child who had run towards him to hug him.

'Not like? I'm just floored.'

'Why couldn't you have said this before? Why wait for me to ask?'

'Everything looks good on you, Sugi. I was searching for words…that's all.'

'Nice excuse.' She lisped, but her face had blossomed again at Natesan's praise. Natesan looked away, feeling something choke inside him. He gathered himself. 'Do you know how proud I am of my wife? Just watch. Today every guest is going to be jealous of me. They'll think this old man has struck gold!'

'Nooo…you are not an old man.' Sugandhi moved away quickly. He could only see the back of her flushed neck, the ring of flowers around her hair and the curve of her legs below her back.

Maybe he shouldn't have commented on his age? Which young woman would want to hear her husband utter those words? Is that why the light that shone in the moss green had blown out? Did the gold dim too? Was she angry? Poor child! Child? His wife, his wife and he had tied the tali around her neck.

19

He stood staring at the wall for a while. Then he went to his room and looked at the map of the forest areas he had to inspect the next day.

Beyond the forest blossoms that flared in bunches, a jeep stood near the thorny fence.

He came out of his room.

'Welcome. Come in.'

An elderly couple and a young man came out of the jeep. The older man had driven the jeep.

'Vanakkam, vanakkam Amma.'

'Vanakkam. How are you? You look just the same as you did eight years ago,' the woman said.

'No, no, he looks younger,' his friend laughed mischievously.

Natesan's face flushed a bit. Was this a jibe at him for his having married a second time since then?

'You are always ready to tease others…Who is this young man?' Natesan looked at the handsome, well-dressed young man.

'My sister's son, Senthil. He works in Chennai. He came here on work for a week and is returning tomorrow. Since it's a Sunday, he was at home today. I said that you are my friend and persuaded him to come along.'

After the introductions they went into the living room.

'Sugi! Where are you? The guests have come.'

Then he remembered that she was a bit upset when she had gone inside. Was she still angry? No, she looked quite normal when she came in. Wow! Exquisite beauty walked in with her. The first three Azhvars[1] are supposed to have felt an all-pervading presence crowding them in the small space. The sweep of her beauty too pervaded the whole room, leaving them breathless.

After this thought flashed through his mind, he saw her as a person and saw that she was apprehensive and hesitant. The young wife was worried. She stood like a student waiting for her results, waiting for her husband's friends to approve of her – a punishment for her youth?

'My wife, Sugandhi.' His voice melted with tenderness towards her. 'This is Vedachalam. I have often spoken to you of him, haven't I? When I was working in the north on a project, he was the auditor. He is a very close friend. We are meeting again after eight years, because we have been shuffled around by transfers. The other day, as I was returning home, I happened to see him. I took his address and invited him. That is his wife and the young man is his sister's son. He works in Chennai.'

He gave this long introduction hoping that it would give her time to overcome her shyness. But it did not seem to work. She looked a bit scared. Her smile too was strained and beads of perspiration dotted her forehead like heat rash.

'Vanakkam, please come.' She folded her hands in welcome, but her voice was very low.

The guests gave her a once over. The faintly jealous expression in Vedachalam's eyes was testimony to her beauty. His wife, Kamalam, knew Natesan's first wife. She may have looked upon Sugandhi as a usurper who had taken over her friend's place, but it was not evident in her expression as she handed Sugandhi a small plastic basket. There were oranges inside it and Sugandhi made a sound of protest as she took it.

'Please take them. I can't come to meet a new bride empty-handed.'

'Thanks.'

'Let's sit down for a chat. Sugi, keep the fruit here – we can even have the fruit while talking.'

Sugandhi placed the fruit basket on a table. And they sat down on the chairs. Sugandhi sat next to Kamalam. It was then she noticed that Senthil, who sat on the sofa across, was looking at her. Looking at her intensely...For how long? And staring at another man's wife...a stranger...Would anyone do it? Rogue! She was angry and uncomfortable. She turned to Kamalam.

'What is your native place, dear?' At this question from Kamalam, Sugandhi said hesitantly, 'Amma would say we came from somewhere near Coimbatore. But as long as I remember, we have been in Chennai.'

'Then your native place is Chennai.'

Sugandhi smiled. She patted her face with her handkerchief. The breeze had turned chilly. Was it going to rain again? She looked out of the window. No, it was not raining. When she turned her head, her eyes fell on Senthil. She quickly turned away.

How he stares. He is young and of her generation. That is why he stares like that.

Her discomfort increased, her heart beat fast and her cheeks turned red.

'Don't misunderstand me for calling you "nee". You are very much younger than me. So I can't call you "neenga", as I called her.'

As soon as she said 'her', Kamalam bit her tongue at her own tactlessness. But Sugandhi seemed not to have noticed.

'Call me as you did. I am much younger.' As she said this, Sugandhi glanced at Senthil from the corner of her eye, to see if he was still staring at her. Then she looked away.

'What does your father do? Brothers...sisters?'

'Two brothers and two sisters.'

She did not say what her father did. Kamalam thought that obviously he did not do anything worth mentioning. Must be a poor family – five children and she the eldest of a poor family. Kamalam looked at Natesan with a trace of sadness.

For a while the two women did not speak. Natesan was discussing work-related problems with his friend.

'Where do you live in Chennai?'

There was total silence for a moment. Then with a start, Sugandhi realized that the question was directed at her.

When she lifted her head, she saw Senthil's smiling, eager face. The deep voice, which had a lilt to it, sounded like music to her ears.

She could not say anything for a minute. Then a thrill ran through her. Her face felt hot, as though a flame had been held near it.

'Mrs Natesan, where in Chennai is your house?' Senthil repeated the question. It was an ordinary, casual question. But it filled her with joy. The breeze blew in with an intimacy and it was as if a screen lifted to reveal a friend's face.

'Ranganathan Street, Mambalam.' She struggled to say these words.

'We are in Karunanidhi Nagar.'

'I don't know all those areas.'

'It's a new colony. Now on the bus route.'

'I have not gone to Chennai since I got married.'

Silence again. Then she continued, 'Now there are many new areas.'

'Yes, many nagars. Shastri Nagar, Besant Nagar, Indira Nagar, and Vallalar Nagar instead of Mint Street.'

'I know Besant Nagar. My friend lives there. She writes to me. A very rich girl.'

The conversation stopped. She felt she had talked too much.

What will he think?

Now Kamalam joined the conversation.

'How do you spend your time here? It is a forest area and not developed yet.'

'Kamalam, that has its own charm. Nature is unspoilt. Just look at this house. It looks like a lovely hermitage – so peaceful.'

'That is fine for us older people. She is young and will need some entertainment.'

Vedachalam felt that his wife had referred to Sugandhi's age unthinkingly. He looked at Natesan anxiously. But Natesan was smiling.

'Do you know there is a ladies' club here? I have made her a member. There is a radio at home. There are only two houses here with an electric connection. Sometimes when I am free, we go to the movies. Tell them, Sugi,' said Natesan.

'Yes, there is radio and cinema. And time passes.'

'Oh, you have a cinema too?' asked Senthil.

'There is, and you have to go up and down in the jeep for half an hour. They show only old movies. Sometimes, the reel gets cut. We have sent them a request from the Ladies' Club to screen new films,' Sugandhi answered. As she spoke, she felt the sweetness of the joy rising within her. How attentively he listened to her!

'*Bobby* is doing very well in Chennai. You must come there at least to watch it,' Senthil laughed.

'Even if I have not seen the movie, I listen to the songs often on the radio.'

'Do you like film songs?'

'Mmm, yes I do…to listen and to even sing.'

'Sing? Can you sing, Sugi? I never knew all these days,' said Natesan sounded astonished.

Sugandhi was surprised into silence. It was true, he did not know. She had not told him. Why had she said it at this time…? Without even realizing it, why had she now recalled all her talents and interests so effortlessly?

'Why don't you sing a song now?' asked Kamalam.

'Not a song from *Bobby*, please. I am just sick and tired of them,' said Vedachalam.

'Any Tamizh song?' suggested Kamalam.

25

Sugandhi looked up with hesitation. Senthil was still staring at her, but it did not annoy her now.

'Please sing, Amma,' said Kamalam.

Senthil's eyes were fixed on her, they were bright and brimming with expectation. She felt a stirring in her heart. She turned to her husband and he said, 'Sing, Sugi.'

'Is it okay if I sing a film song?' Sugandhi asked Kamalam. 'Sure.'

She sang *'Ezhu swarangalukkul ethanai paadal'*.

At first her voice was low and trembling. Gradually it gained strength and her heart, soul and emotions blended into one. The whole world was in her being, her music and an eager face in front.

When the song ended, the guests showered compliments on her. Suddenly she felt shy, and blushing, bent her head down. As moss covers the clear water, she covered herself with the pallu of her moss green sari.

'Sugi, I never knew you could sing so beautifully.'

She looked up with a jerk. Was it a compliment or a complaint?

'Do you sing pop music? Do you know "Enjoy yourself, it is later than you think" and all that?' asked Senthil.

'I don't know all that,' Sugandhi bent her head down again.

'Sugi, did you learn music formally from a teacher? Do you know devotional songs too?'

'I just sing. Haven't learnt singing formally. Whatever I sing is just from listening. If a good musician sang at a concert hall like Vani Mahal, they would take me.' What started as a reply to her husband ended as an explanation to Senthil.

Time went by as they sat chatting.

'Sugi, why don't you serve the snacks?'

'Why take all this trouble?' objected Vedachalam.

'Very nice. Does anyone let the guests go without serving them anything?'

'Please have the fruit first. I will get the snacks.' Sugandhi got up and placed the oranges in front of them.

'Why have the fruit now? We are anyway going to have the snacks.'

'Will you get indigestion if you have a fruit too?' Sugandhi smiled and pushed the fruit closer to him. Senthil did not refuse this time. Sugandhi brought a cardboard box and placed it on a stool for them to throw the peels into. The stool was the closest to Senthil's seat. Senthil smiled at her. She went inside with a spring in her gait. She sensed that his eyes were following her as she went in, and she walked as if she were dancing.

She went to the kitchen and looked at the masal vadais she had made earlier. She had kept them warm.

Does he like masal vadais? Would it have been better if she had made puri-potato?

She felt a pang of regret that there was no wheat flour at home today. But the regret disappeared when she saw the Mohandal…golden-yellow mouth-watering squares. She was glad that she had made Mohandal and not the common rava kesari or peanut candy that everyone makes.

As she was placing the sweet, vadai and chutney on

the plates, something occurred to her and she went to the bathroom. Though this was not the time, she washed her face with soap and water, then looked at herself in the mirror and powdered her face. Instead of the round dot on her forehead, she drew an attractive tilakam. She was particularly happy about the gold necklace. She dusted off the powder from her sari and carefully examined whether the powder on her face was patchy. She stared at her own beauty in the mirror. There was a thrill of excitement in her heart. Then she hastened to the kitchen, put the snacks on a wooden tray and walked to the living room.

Senthil and Kamalam stood up as soon as she came in. Kamalam went up to her and said, 'Please give me the tray.'

'No, that is okay.'

She placed the tray on the centre table and served the guests. First Kamalam, then Vedachalam and Natesan. Finally, when she came to Senthil, she asked with slight concern, 'I hope you like masal vadai?'

'I love to eat, and I like everything.'

'Oh, is that why you refused oranges?' she asked playfully.

Senthil laughed and bit into the sweet. 'Oh! Delicious!'

'I made it myself. It's a new dish – Mohandal.'

'I think you can call it Manamohandal.'

Sugandhi's eyes sparkled, her cheeks went pink and she smiled as if a thousand chandeliers had been lit up. She turned to the others and asked if everything was fine. She noticed that her husband's eyes were on her, even though he was talking to his friends. Was he surprised that she had touched up her face? She looked down.

'Just a minute.' She went in to bring water and then went in again. Kamalam followed her to help her with the coffee.

'Mrs Natesan, you should not have taken so much trouble. We are strangers to you, but Natesan and I are like brothers. There is no need for all this formality.'

'That's okay. I'm very happy you all came.'

'It's not that, Mrs Natesan.'

'You can call me just Sugandhi, I am younger than you.' Then she quickly looked at her husband's face with a flash of nervousness and bent her head down.

Vedachalam turned to his friend and asked. 'How long will you be here?'

'Only the preliminary work is over. Now we have to choose a site to build the bridge and then clear the trees. I will know by and by.'

The conversation turned to general topics and all of them joined in. It was getting dark. Sugandhi switched on the light. The guests got up to leave.

'So, we will take our leave.'

'You are going?' asked Sugandhi.

'Come over soon,' Kamalam invited them.

They all stepped out and there was still some sunlight. Natesan and Sugandhi accompanied the guests as they walked to the jeep parked outside the fence. It so happened that Vedachalam, Kamalam and Natesan went ahead, while Senthil and Sugandhi trailed behind.

'I'm very happy I came, Mrs Natesan.'

Sugandhi did not say anything. Inside her, some emotion knotted up like a ball.

'Will you come to our house?'

'If he takes me there,' she said softly.

'I'll leave day after tomorrow.'

She bit her lower lip. Both of them remained silent. He kept looking at her sideways as they walked. Her face was flushed and she was afraid even to breathe.

'You sang beautifully.'

Senthil sang the song softly under his breath. Without realizing it, she hummed along. Their voices blended in unison. She looked up at him and smiled, as though plunged in ecstatic joy. Then the voices died down. The young man and woman walked along, their footsteps in matching rhythm.

The jeep drove away after the formal farewells. Beyond the casuarina trees in that woody region stood silver oak trees and the jeep disappeared beyond their leaves, which shone like pale gold.

Sugandhi felt as if the world had suddenly become empty, bereft of beauty and charm. A heavy load weighed her down. She felt like casting away her new clothes, as well as her necklace and her tilakam, and sitting there slowly dissolving in the darkness.

She turned to Natesan. He was looking at her…he seemed older than ever before.

Something pierced Sugandhi's heart. Her lips wobbled and the sorrow of an unbearable guilt engulfed her; she started to weep.

Natesan patted her back, hugged her and stroked her hair. 'Don't cry, Sugi. The fault is not yours. Don't cry.'

Dusk darkened into night. She was still sobbing and he was still comforting her.

three

A Good Friend

Neela thought that happiness was the best cosmetic aid when she looked at Madhuri. It was as if all the loveliness that Madhuri had yearned for was now radiating from her face, and in a moment she had bloomed with beauty!

'Hello! You look so happy! Are you going to get married or something?' Neela asked her friend, with a smile.

'Is marriage the only reason for a woman to be happy? Have a sweet; I have something to celebrate!' the 'new' beauty said.

'That is why I asked, what is the reason?'

'Tell me what my name is.'

'What is this riddle? What do you mean?'

'W-h-a-t i-s m-y n-a-m-e?'

'Till today, I was under the impression that it is Madhuri. Have you changed it or what? Haven't seen the newspaper yet.'

'What name did you say?'

'Madhuri. Madhuri. Or Madhuri Alagesan, right?'

'Wrong.'

'What else?'

'Dr Madhuri Alagesan.'

'What? Got your PhD?'

'Congratulations!' This came after a second's silence.

'Thank you, Neela.'

Neela hugged her friend...but struggled to say something.

'Very...happy. When did you get the news?'

'Yesterday.'

'Good...unofficial, is it?'

'No no, I was personally intimated by the university.'

'Oh...that it has been accepted for PhD?'

'Yes.'

'I see...very happy. What did you say the subject of your thesis was? I have forgotten...Who can remember all this?'

'The Image of Women in the Indian Epics.'

'Now you will proudly write "Dr" before your name...Good, good. Being unmarried, you have achieved this, at least.'

Madhuri looked up at her and smiled.

'Your guide, Professor Pazhanivel, is unmarried, no Madhuri?'

'Yes, why?'

'No...I heard that he likes women.'

'Really?'

'My uncle told me...You know, his son did not get a medical seat. Another boy got it through the recommendation of a member of the Assembly.'

'Really?'

'Today everything happens only by recommendation. I am not saying you got your doctorate like that. Generally that is how it happens. You are intelligent. Don't I know that?'

'Will you have some coffee?'

'It will taste bitter after the sweet…Then…Madhuri, how old would Professor Pazhanivel be? Roughly fifty?'

'Maybe.'

'What does he look like?'

'He looks like a fifty-year-old.' Madhuri sat on the divan.

'Good joke…You must have gone to him often to discuss things with him to seek his advice in connection with the research. That would have been some timepass. Now it will be difficult to pass the time…a pity.'

Madhuri picked up a *Reader's Digest* and leaned back on the divan.

'Why I said that was if you had family, husband and children, time would just fly by. You don't have all that, no?'

'Yes.'

'If you had all that, why would you burden yourself with a PhD, research and all that kind of rubbish?'

'So according to you, Neela, no woman would want to pursue education as an end in itself, right?'

'Don't worry, Madhuri. A girl I know got married at thirty-two. At thirty-two, you can't call her a girl, she is a Maami – an older woman. You will be thirty next month, on the fourth. That's not too late.'

'Not bad. You remember my birthday.'

'Aren't you my friend? How can I forget?'

'That's true. I'm one year older than you.'

'One year, four months and eleven days.'

'Now will you have coffee? It may taste less bitter.' Madhuri laughed.

'Let it be. What is the hurry? The sweet was nice. Was it from Bombay Mithaiwala?'

'Made at home.'

'Really? Wonderful. You will do research and also cooking? Hmm…You will also feel bad. You can only serve your dishes to your friends. I'm sure you wish you had children for whom you could cook a variety of dishes. Can you play with a PhD degree like a child? Or tie it like a tali around your neck? Don't worry, Madhuri. When the time comes, you will also get married. I will look out for you too.'

'Thank you.'

'If you don't mind, give me four of those sweets in a plastic bag. I'll tell them that Madhuri Maami gave them. Don't misunderstand me for calling you Maami. It's only then that the children will understand. Vanitha loves sweets, will just gobble them up. I keep telling her that no one will marry her if her teeth go bad. But does she listen? Maybe she too will remain unmarried and do research like you. Who knows? Her father will just die.'

'I'll pack the sweets for them.'

'Dr Madhuri Alagesan. I, too, would have done my doctorate. But my parents got me married soon after BA because my in-laws were so keen. Is it easy to study after that? But I have no regrets. Do you know how happy I am? My in-laws are so fond of me. My parents-in-law call me for everything, and for my sister-in-law and brothers-in-law, my word is law. And then there are my two darling children. My husband cannot be away from me even for a minute. He needs me beside him to get everything ready till he goes for work. In the evening, I must be there to receive him with a smile. Or else he will shamelessly shout in front of everyone, "Where is my darling reception committee?" I just die of embarrassment! Even now, on most days when he comes home from work, he gets me flowers, fruits or sweets. If I tell him he should not buy things just for me when there are elders and children at home, he whispers in my ear, "But you alone are my wife!" He is terrible, Madhuri! Day and night he needs me. But poor thing, you will not understand that…'

Neela keenly looked at her friend. Madhuri was unruffled. Neela sat next to her with a sigh of disappointment.

'Dr Madhuri Alagesan. Is your thesis very long? Give it to me. I'll try to read it when I have time.'

'Of course, I will, and you tell me what you think.'

'Why do you need my opinion, now that you have got your doctorate?…By the way, what does your professor say? He would have conveyed his good wishes with happiness, right? Be careful when you are with him. Please don't think who I am to advise you. I know I am only a BA, not a PhD like you. But you don't know the world…not having married. So though I am younger, I have more experience. That is why I ask you to be careful with him. He has a weakness for women. Though you are not a young girl, you are still a woman. You'll have so many deep desires. You must have had to meet him often, isn't it? I am sure you like your professor very much…?'

'Meaning?'

'Che, not in a "bad" sense. I have heard he is very intelligent. My brother-in-law listened to his lectures when he did his MA. I have heard him say that he is very intelligent. That is why I asked if you liked him…And what have you written in your thesis? Is it about who is the best among the epic women?'

'Yes. Mainly Draupadi.'

'Why? Is it because she had five husbands? You must be having a complex.' Neela said with a sly smile.

'Not because she married five men, but about her bond with Krishna.'

'Oh! Her devotion?'

'I think it is more a special friendship than devotion. What an example of a friendship between a man and a woman. There are no sexual overtones, but a pure, intellectual friendship between two equal human beings. Theirs is not the traditionally accepted man–woman relationship, like father–daughter, husband–wife or brother–sister. Theirs is a relationship that rejects the stupid misconception that if an unrelated man and woman are close to each other, it must be for sex. What do you think?'

Neela's face turned red and she looked away.

'Why hasn't the Krishna–Draupadi principle that gives woman the dignity of a fellow human being, never taken root in our society, Neela?'

'What do I know of your big concepts? Am I well-read, like you? Just a mere BA. Okay, okay…you asked me if I will have coffee. I'll have it now. I want something to drink.'

Madhuri went to the kitchen. She looked a vision of loveliness. What an alchemy! Her name would appear in the papers. Neela wiped her face and neck with her sari. It was not even summer and she was perspiring like this! Madhuri brought two tumblers of coffee and gave one to her friend. Neela had a sip.

'Is it okay?'

'How can it be otherwise? After all, it is coffee made by a PhD! Don't be upset. I said it in jest. What next? Marriage, isn't it? In the end, it has to be that?' Neela laughed.

'I want to do some research on the history of the slave trade and the consequences. I'm trying for a scholarship abroad.'

The hand holding the coffee tumbler halted midway.

'Is it easy to get a foreign scholarship?'

'I agree it is not easy, but I thought I'd try.'

Neela resumed drinking her coffee.

'That is true, it can't be a cakewalk.' She flashed an exaggerated smile. 'But you will get it! You're clever. Dr Madhuri Alagesan…hmm, at least this honour…to compensate for having missed marriage.'

The smile faded and the voice dropped.

'Dr Madhuri Alagesan.'

Madhuri's father, Alagesan, had returned from office. 'Hello, Neela! How are you? It has been a long time since you came to this side of town!'

'Don't even ask me, Maama. If you are immersed in family, then you have to think a hundred times before you can go here or there. Even now, I have to get back before my husband returns home. I must give him his coffee and snacks, it can't be otherwise. Then I have to make dinner for my parents-in-law. They love my dishes.' Neela smiled at her friend.

'You're lucky. How are the children?'

'Fine, Maama. Vanitha is always first in her class. Suresh has already started collecting pictures of tennis stars. Maybe he will become a tennis champion in the future! I am so proud of my children. What more can a woman want?'

'Absolutely correct. Tell your friend that. She has finished her doctorate and wants to pursue research. Or else she wants to become a college professor…She wants to write a book…or freelance journalism. She has no interest in getting married. Marriage does not figure in any of her plans!'

'Poor thing! Since she is not married, she's bound to say she is not interested. Would any girl openly say she is pining to get married? She will have to engage herself in research and this and that. What do you say, Madhuri?'

Madhuri did not say anything and just smiled at her.

'It is not that. Won't everyone say that she has no mother and the father doesn't seem to care?'

'Let it be, Maama. Marriage will happen when the time

comes. She is only thirty…just a year older than me.'

'One year, four months and eleven days.'

'Look at her teasing me. I told her not to worry and that a girl I know got married at thirty-two.'

'I hope your words come true.'

'So shall I leave?'

'Are you leaving because I came, Neela? I'll go to my room. Both of you can continue.'

'No, it is getting late. I told you, didn't I, that my husband will be upset if I'm not there to receive him. I came today because I had not seen Madhuri for a long time. And then she surprises me with the news about her doctorate. All this while, I was congratulating her. Okay, bye Maama. Bye Madhuri – sorry, Dr Madhuri PhD.'

'Bye. Take these sweets for your children.' She wanted to add 'from Madhuri Maami', but desisted out of pity for Neela.

Neela left with the sweets.

'Your Neela is a good friend.'

'Yes, Appa…she is.'

four

You Don't Know

Parvatam saw the car even as it turned into her street. As she waited eagerly and saw the cluster of heads in the car, each indistinguishable from the other, she quietened her throbbing heart.

'Be calm, dear heart, joy approaches you once again.'

The throbbing joy shimmied through her as she readied herself, and another part of her mind went through a checklist.

- She had sent an application for two extra tins of milk powder.
- She had organized a young help to babysit (Ganga would surely send her in the evening).
- She had told the cook that the children would need their food earlier.

The taxi halted in front of the house. There arose a self-generated din and Meena's bright smiling face appeared, the tiny voices of the children soft with shyness.

'Come Meena, come children. Hey Balu, the first step is a bit broken. Careful, you may hurt yourself. Meena, give me the baby. Hey Muniyaa, unload the luggage…Meena, you look as if you have lost weight. I hope you are not unwell. The baby looks just like you, only her complexion is like your husband's. Vanitha, careful…hold my hand.'

The words and her warm welcome flowed forth. Where within her lay the source of her joy and enthusiasm? That was a magic spring. Every year, it replenished itself and drenched her this season…the one season which lent meaning to the entire year.

After sending the car away, Meena turned around with words that fell upon her like a shower of rose water.

'Akka! How are you?'

'I'm fine. Nothing wrong. Meena, the little one is very friendly and has come to me, though I'm not familiar to her. Just see how sweetly she is perched on my hip. My golden darling, my sweet one.'

Parvatam hugged the nine-month-old child lovingly. Then she turned to the older ones.

'Mani, are you going to school like a good boy? I'm sure you are the class topper. Balu, how are your car picture books? Vanitha, see, I have got so many chalk pieces, you can scribble on the floor to your heart's content!'

The children stood shyly to one side. These days, Vanitha did not scribble with chalk on the floor. Wasn't she five years old? Balu was now obsessed only with cricket…he was a big boy, all of nine. Was he a kid to stare at car pictures?

42

Mani, the eldest, was the only one to respond with a polite mumble. At fourteen, he was tall and had to bend down to Perimma – mother's elder sister. It was only when she noticed this that Parvatam remembered that she had seen them two years ago. It struck her then that her comments flowing from those memories were out of place. She bit her tongue at the thought of having mentioned the pieces of chalk and car pictures.

Meena laughed heartily.

'Hey kids! If you want to know all our mythological stories, this Perimma is the one – she can just captivate you with her storytelling. Don't leave her, okay?'

The children cast away their momentary hesitation and stood around her in a circle.

'Perimma, will you tell us stories? Lots of them?'

Parvatam looked at her sister gratefully for a minute.

'I'll tell you as many as you want, but first come and have your milk.'

She corrected herself at once.

'Meena, do they now have milk or coffee?'

'Vanitha will have milk and the older ones, coffee.'

'Come along, then, for your coffee and milk.'

'Akka, only for the kids, is it? No coffee or milk for me?' Meena asked teasingly, giving her sister a gentle smile.

At that moment, the universe contained only the two sisters, their eyes filled with love that sprang from within them, watering the roots of their lives and forming a sweet wordless connection which tied them together as one. It left the children aside and even left them forgotten. The bond between the siblings was very special – dearer than the bonds that are formed later with a partner or a child, however necessary and precious these might be. It was a bond that was not artificial or deliberate; it was born of its own – a divine feeling that encompasses one regardless of age or status.

'Hmm, these are not for you. I will only give you delicious Bournvita,' Parvatam laughed.

Her face was transformed by a glow that sprang from an old source, while her age and widowhood slipped away.

The sisters laughed. The children could not comprehend the moment, except that they felt they had been somehow excluded and this made them a wee bit jealous. They joined in the laughter anyway.

That evening, Parvatam spent just ten minutes with her friend, Ganga, in the park.

'My sister, Meena, and her children have come. The house is lively, the children want me to tell them stories. Meena teases me about my not giving her coffee or milk. See you, Ganga…no time at all.'

Kamala and Meena would visit their sister every alternate year during the holidays with their children and spend some time with her. If their husbands could take leave from work, they would accompany them. This year, Meena's husband could not come. At such times, just the sister and children would come. It was not that they felt that in the absence of parents or a brother, they needed a place to relax in, as if it were their mother's home. The truth was that they came because they were bound by their love for their sister to do this as a duty.

Who did Parvatam have except her sisters? There was a husband. And then he died. It was a dream, an old blurred dream. The distance created by time had blunted even the pain and what remained was only a trace of that thought, which arose as a matter of reflex. It was a pain of years past, when she gave up wearing the kumkum dot on her forehead and flowers in her hair, as was the custom. Parvatam had not forgotten that pain. But she would put it away in the loft, along with her Ramayana books that she read every day and the handicraft that was her hobby, when she prepared the house to receive her sister and her children with happy expectation, elaborate arrangements and easy smiles.

When the annual visitors left, she would again accept the pain of her loneliness, her constant companion. The house was hers only to receive her sisters in turn. The house throbbed with life only during the one-and-a-half or two months that they were there. That was the time which gave meaning to her life, the harvest season. The other ten months the house lay fallow. Parvatam did not think this was wrong. Could one attain fulfilment in life only as a wife, husband, mother or child? Could one not attain fulfilment as an Akka – elder sister? Born as the eldest of three daughters to parents without sons, married at sixteen and letting go of her childhood, losing her married life in two months, as if that was the last doll slipping through her fingers, she was perhaps meant to be just such an Akka, thought Parvatam.

Her memory of her parents was sharper than her memory of her husband.

They were alive till her twenty-fifth year. Appa left first, Amma followed the next year. As though reluctant to leave her widowed daughter, who had no support, Amma fought a slow battle with her disease and little by little, her life was defeated and ended. Parvatam would sometimes yearn for her voice, sometimes for the kind and gentle look that would suffuse her face. In the long sleepless nights, when her aimless heart would grow heavy with listlessness and emptiness, her hand would grope for Amma's touch, which had gone forever. Shrunken and grey at forty, she was a symbolic mother's refuge for her sisters, with whom she roused herself to enthusiasm. Yearning to be young and a child again, her eyes would search for Appa's touch all around and above and in every empty bit of the air. But this was only for a short time. The love among the sisters was deep. She did feel a sense of fulfilment when opening the doors, waiting to welcome her sisters. At other times, she had her books and her craft to fill her life. In the softness of that flowering, Ganga's friendship was the fragrant pollen.

Ganga lived two miles away. As she was not married, her age had been thirty for several years. She believed that the privilege of revealing one's age came like the mangalsutra with marriage. She and Parvatam were close friends. Burdened by her single status and feeling a vague discontent caused by the ache, Ganga took vicarious pleasure in listening to someone else's experiences. She had many friends. She would let them talk while she listened, her expression conveying her keen interest. This interest would be manifested sometimes as pity, sometimes jealousy and sometimes contempt. She reserved the last for Parvatam. Ganga thought that the way Parvatam spoke of her sisters and their families – with love and not a trace of envy – was despicable. Seeking a life of her own, she thought that living vicariously off the lives of others displayed a lack of self-worth. This contempt was not visible to others. She would give her friend whatever help she needed, but in her heart she harboured contempt.

Parvatam and she met every evening at a park nearby. Parvatam would narrate the day's events to her. If her sisters were visiting her, Parvatam would not spend too much time with her. Yet she did not forget her friend and their time together. She would come in a rush, with a quick smile, and she would recount what had happened that day, as though a switch had been turned on.

'Today, I sent Mani and Balu to a morning show with the neighbours. What a ruckus the kid, Vanitha, made because of that! Very intelligent!'

'Today, Meena insisted that she would make the afternoon coffee. It was divine.'

'The little one, Sachu, is so smart, you know? She has seen the postman coming home every day. Today, he went past because there was no letter for me. You know what this mite did? She stretches her hand out, saying, "Mmm…," asking for the letter! How do you like that! Can't speak yet, but she has a head full of brains.'

'You know what Meena said? "Akka, Kamala and I have no cares because we know we can ask you for anything we need. If you were not there, what would we have done?" Will the world come to an end if I am not there? It is just her affection for me which makes her think that way.'

'Today there was a letter from Kamala. Meena and I read it together. It was as if Kamala was right there with us.'

'Ganga, guess what? Today Meena was serving me my lunch. This fellow, Mani, says that his mother loves her sister more than her children.'

'You know Ganga, this Meena insists that I should feed her children. Normally, however much one loves someone, one would not like to let another feed one's children.' Because one suspects that others will not do it the right way. But my sister has such confidence in me.'

These daily reports, brief and swift, would carry varied messages with a half-hidden pride echoing through them. Ganga felt a distaste when she saw this happiness and pride transforming the scrawny, withered form that was Parvatam. Her heart curled with contempt but her mouth sparkled with the words. 'Hmm, is that so?' and, 'How loving,' to goad Parvatam.

'Yes, Ganga. Every morning when I wake up, I am filled with joy at this wealth of affection and good fortune. Okay, see you.'

'But you came just now.' Ganga would address her with the term of respect to indicate that she was much younger than Parvatam. 'Why do you want to rush off at once? Can't you relax a little in the park?'

'No time. I have to go home and continue with the narration of stories to the children. It is the story of legendary King Karthaveeryarjuna, and Meena too wants to listen, like a kid. After they leave, anyway it will be back to you and me. See you.'

The days dawned in enthusiasm, continued in joy and set in contentment. The joy that her sister and her children brought was returned in full measure and shared with them, and she savoured that sweetness.

That day too dawned like any other day; she spent the whole day playing with the children and chatting with Meena. The conversation between the two sisters was the manifestation of a closeness that was something quite apart from the children. Just as two persons would exchange an intimate glance over the heads of others who would not know that this was a bond of love which was theirs alone.

In the evening, Parvatam brought snacks, coffee and milk from the kitchen for everyone. After taking care of the other children, Meena filled Sachu's bottle with milk and went out to wash her hands. Parvatam sat Sachu down on her lap to feed her. Every day, it was Meena who gave the bottle to the baby.

The child, who had been playing with a rubber doll till then, had four gulps hastily as she was hungry, and then struggled free to start playing again.

'Come darling, finish the milk.'

The child paid no heed and crawled some distance, sat up and looked around.

'Come here and drink the milk, my child.'

The child located the rubber doll and with a loud gurgle, rushed towards it.

Parvatam stood up and went near her, and gently pulled her close.

'My sweet one, you can play after you drink this.'

Sachu wriggled away. She crawled sideways and when she reached the doll, her mouth opened with joy.

'Hold the doll and drink, okay? Your little tummy will feel hungry and cry…' Parvatam forced the child's head down and stuck the bottle into her mouth.

Sachu howled but did not drink. The milk squirted out of the bottle teat in a white spray all over her head. She shook her head this way and that and tried to get up, kicking her legs. Meena, who came in just then, did not know what was happening.

'Akka, are you feeding her? Why is she not drinking?'

'She wants to play and does not care if she is hungry. Just a baby. Here Sachu, are you going to be a good baby or not? Come, my little dove, my doll.'

'Again the struggle, the fuss.' Meena bent down.

'Mmmmaa, mmaa…' Sachu tried to get up, weeping all the while. Again, the bottle pressed against her lips, the milk came out in a thick spurt, the child choked and began to cough.

'Akka, let her go for a while.'

'If she throws a tantrum, can we let her go? Just now…she will drink.'

Parvatam pressed the child's head with her left hand, and with the right, held the bottle firmly to the mouth of the child, who wanted to slip out. The child choked and spluttered. Parvatam was scared and pulled the bottle away, and then she heard Meena's voice.

'You don't know how to do it, Akka, give her to me.'

Parvatam's hands dropped limply at this blow, which struck her deep in the heart. She saw from afar, as though in a dream, Meena laying the child on her lap and giving her the bottle gently, and the child drinking the milk quietly. Parvatam sat with her back to Meena, her head bent down, as she shivered within and her body went numb. Something choked her throat, while her heart beat faster than ever. She perspired all over, but her lips were dry. Something trickled down her cheek into her mouth and it was salty...tears or sweat?

Why didn't she move? What was this sudden heaviness in her heart? Is that why she could not move?

'You don't know how to do it, Akka.'

Why did the heart sob with pain at these words? It was only Meena who had said them. Meena, her dear sister who poured love on her, had said this casually. She would not have said this to hurt her or insult her. It was clear that she did not comprehend the impact of her words as she continued with her everyday, commonplace chatter.

'...After that when I went to the movie with our guests...'

What was she saying? Something in passing, about some experience of hers...nothing registered in Parvatam's brain.

51

'You don't know how to do it, Akka.' These were the words that kept echoing densely inside her without ceasing.

For some reason, it sounded like a small but sharp comment on Parvatam's entire life. Truths which she knew but had not faced – that her life was an empty loneliness, that it was a long journey without a child or any joy – rushed towards her like waves, like serial chains that dragged the mountains behind a rolling rock. A searing burn on her soul... she could not bear it. She slowly got up, but her feet faltered.

'Akka... are you unwell?' Meena put the child down abruptly and got up in alarm and hugged her. The loving sister, there was no fault in her love. Her hand had struck the blow without knowing! But... the blow still hurt.

'Nothing, Meena.' She could not explain it. However strong the love may be or close the bond, a screen had come down between them – a screen that resulted from a difference between them. Meena would be very upset if she knew. She must not tell her, she could not tell her.

'Nothing, Meena.' She slowly went out of the room as the gloom surrounded her on all four sides.

As usual, she went to the park at five in the evening, but the dark gloom spread on her face. Her heart was tired. She sat on the bench.

Ganga came and sat next to her. The fact that Parvatam was sitting down indicated that she was not going to just stand there, reel off the day's events and rush away. Ganga's contempt sharpened as she was sure that something special was up today.

'What's the matter, Parvatam?' she asked with a deceptive smile.

Parvatam looked up. Her eyes shone with unshed tears. Her frame was bent, her face drooping, and her slightly open lips trembled. Her emotions gathered near her lips, but she did not say a word.

'Tell me please. What happened today? Didn't your sister or the children say anything?'

Parvatam shrank within herself. Hadn't her sister said anything?

'You don't know how to do it, Akka.'

Didn't she have something to tell Ganga? But could she repeat Meena's words? How could she tell Ganga that her dear sister had hurt her deeply? Had Meena done it on purpose? Moreover, she too should not have fed that child by force. Frankly, what did she know about all this? How could she get angry? Meena had not said it deliberately, nor without reason. There was no untruth in her love for her Akka. Parvatam was aware of that. Her heart's tears were her private grief. If she held Meena responsible for that, it would be ingratitude. It was all right to broadcast her sister's love for her, but to tell Ganga about this would be a betrayal.

'Nothing, Ganga.'

'That is not true. Something has happened today.'

'I told you nothing happened.'

'Then why do you look like this?'

'Headache.'

'Lies. You are hiding something from me.'

53

'So what if I am hiding something?' Parvatam said with intensity. 'Am I bound to tell you everything that happens at home? I will tell you if I want to, and if I don't want to, I will never tell you. Understand?'

Parvatam swiftly walked out of the park.

Ganga sat in astonishment. For the first time, she felt a respect for this new assertive Parvatam.

Parvatam walked around aimlessly for a while and when she returned home, the children and Meena were waiting for her at the door.

'Where have you been Akka? It was getting late and I was so worried.' Meena's voice carried the same love and concern as always. Parvatam stood looking at her.

'Perimma, I'm hungry.' That was the little girl, Vanitha.

'Meena, why don't you give the children their food?' Parvatam asked hesitantly.

'Why? Won't you do it? You have fed them with so much love that the children look so much better now.'

A smile began to form on Parvatam's lips. Her heart lightened a bit. The ache in her heart settled itself somewhere inside and subsided a bit. She had to swallow it and go on.

'Come on kids, let us eat.' The voice had the same special love. 'After that, you and I will eat together Meena.'

Parvatam went in.

She was Akka again. That was her joy and her life.

five

Just Like Him

VIJAYA REPLACED THE TELEPHONE receiver in anger.
'Amma! Appa phoned. It seems that fellow is coming home with him for lunch.' Anger and sadness spread over her face. She suppressed the urge to hug her mother and cry aloud.

Gowri went pale. She stood motionless, not knowing what to say.

'Doesn't he care at all about you?' Vijaya murmured softly.
'Here? For lunch?'
'Yes…we have to get a banquet ready for him!'
'I thought he was trying for a job…'
'I believe he has got it. Of course, with Appa's recommendation he would, right? It seems he arrived here this morning. I believe our job is over with this lunch, since he has booked into a hotel tonight.'

Why didn't he go right away to that hotel then? The same

thought crossed the minds of mother and daughter.

'How can Appa be so heartless? How brazen!'

'This is his house and he has the right to invite anyone. How can we get angry?'

'Amma!' Vijaya shouted in shock.

'But…how did that fellow agree to this?' Gowri said thoughtfully, and fell silent.

Vijaya's eyes were wet. Why does a woman avoid criticizing her husband, however wrong he may be, shifting the blame on others? Is she generous or just unaware?

'He is at fault, too. But I am more furious with Appa. How did he have the heart to suggest this? This…isn't this an insult to you? Doesn't it mean he has no respect for you?'

Gowri shrank at this. She clutched at her heart.

'What is this, Amma? Is your heart paining? Amma!'

Gowri's pain overflowed when her daughter rushed to hug her.

'How can you stand this? Poor Amma, just lean on me…'

'I think I will rest now. I feel uneasy.'

Gowri gently released herself from her daughter's clasp and went in. This heart ailment raising its head every now and then…whenever something upset her. She was not afraid to die. But she must live as long as possible for Chandru's sake.

The moment she thought of him, instead of lying down, Gowri went and sat on the floor near Chandru. She stretched her legs and closing her eyes, leant against the wall. Her face reflected all her anxiety.

'What, Amma? Why do you look worried?'

Gowri opened her eyes. The pain in her heart had not subsided. With quivering lips, she looked at her son. A young man of twenty, he was two years older than Vijaya. How sad that he was confined to the bed with a disability affecting his legs, when he should have been enjoying life to the fullest. From his fifth year, when life had dealt him a cruel blow, she had carried him lovingly in her heart. Her concern, her sorrow, her care and her protection wound densely around him and him alone. She had not thought much even about her daughter. She only yearned to live as long as she could for him, as his mother, as his fortress of love.

'What Amma?' Chandru asked.

'Nothing, my dear.'

'Does your chest ache?'

'Yes.'

'Why don't you lie down? Vijaya will take care of you. Rest a bit, Amma.'

'Will lying down now heal my heartache?'

This had never happened before. Sambasivam had never let his other life intrude into this house. It was not that Gowri was unaware of his affairs. Even the talk of that "marriage" had fallen on her ears. The woman in her had risen in rage. Even then – at that young age – she had accepted this stab at her heart and had distanced herself. It was possible for her to do that because he did not fail in fulfilling his obligations towards her and their children, nor did he let his other entanglements offend her dignity. Whenever she saw her disabled son, she would fume. How *can* he…have the heart to do this? The years had rolled by like this.

Chandru knew about his father, but being immobile, had made reading books an excuse for being totally absorbed in himself. To him, it even seemed that there was a certain dignity in Sambasivam's behaviour because he never tried to hide this matter from them, though there was no open scandal. Nor did Gowri deny this. But her apparent acceptance did not last long. She could be indifferent as long as it was about some 'other woman'. But since the day she had learnt that he had had a child with the other woman, a part of her heart had turned to stone. It seemed as if something that was a wispy shadow had suddenly acquired an undeniable, tangible form. He had not received her forgiveness after that. She lived in that house with him, accepting him as her children's father, with nothing more between them than the facade of a marriage.

That peace had been disrupted today. He had invited…the other child, now a young man, for lunch to *this* house. The house where she, *Gowri*, lived! Though she had not openly accepted what Vijaya had said, she had the same feeling. What deep humiliation he had inflicted on her! What heartlessness!

I can't prevent him from inviting that boy here. But I will not see him. Who can compel me to see him? If he owns this house…I do too.

Chandru was surprised to see his mother's face turning red with rage, grief and hatred.

'What is it, Amma? Something has disturbed you, I can see that.'

'Chandru! I too have rights here…What does your father think of himself?'

'Amma!'

Gowri's chest heaved rapidly. Her husband's callousness spread its bitterness in her heart afresh. She stroked her son's legs with vehemence, as though her husband had just then betrayed her. How did he have the heart…when he had a son like this?

'Amma, what happened today? Please tell me.' Chandru raised himself from the pillow, leaning on his elbow, and grasped her shoulder.

Her vehemence subsided. She looked at him with anxiety. He was a man. At that moment, the fact that he was a man and she a woman and, therefore, they were different, created an odd distance between them, separating them beyond the reality of his being her disabled child – the object of her care and concern. She hid her rising emotions.

'Just that my chest hurts too much, Chandru. I will lie down. Don't stop reading. What book is that?'

She did not hear his answer and went upstairs to rest.

Downstairs, Vijaya will instruct the cook what to make for lunch.

Ayyo, why does it hurt like this?

Dear god! Don't take me so soon. I must live long for Chandru's sake, even if I suffer.

Time went by.

59

'Amma, Appa has come with him. Appa was asking where you are.' Vijaya entered the room.

For a moment, Gowri felt as if she was on fire. He…already here…in this house?

'I'm not going down, Vijaya. Tell Appa that my chest is paining a lot.'

'That's right, Amma. Why should you come to see him? If Appa is shameless…'

'Che, shut up. Don't talk like this of Appa. It really hurts, go and tell him.'

Vijaya realized that there was a line she could never cross. She went away.

The tick-tock of the clock hit her like whip strokes. Her chest ached less, but the heartache was unbearable.

The low murmur of conversation from the dining room downstairs could be heard here too.

He was eating in her house. At this moment, he must be relishing the avakkai pickle she had made – for her children.

In a way, her attitude appeared strange even to herself. Why this tumult at this age? Today's incident was just a sequel to what had happened so long ago. Yet, he was here in her house…something that had never happened. He was her husband's son, just like Chandru. It was this thought that made it intolerable. The knowledge was nothing new, but the hurt had surfaced afresh today.

Please let him go away soon.

She heard footsteps on the stairs. As she looked up, she saw Sambasivam.

'Gowri!'

Slight anger in his voice…but she did not reply.

'You deliberately recorded your protest by not coming down, no?'

There was no reply to this either.

'How long would it have taken me to bring him upstairs?'

Her lips trembled and the tears flowed into her heart.

'Has this ever happened? Just this one occasion…'

'I did not want to see his face. I shake all over at the very thought. Do you think what you did was right? Isn't there a hotel here?'

'This house…'

'Lunch over, isn't it? What more? Just go out with your…' She could not utter the word; it burst forth as a sob.

'Finally you have proved you are a mere woman with all her pettiness.'

'If you had considered me a woman, you would not have done this.'

'Forget it. Where is the paakku? That's why I came up. It's not there downstairs. Venu must have paakku after food.' How casually he said it. Venu…That name was new to her, but came naturally to him. Venu…

Chandru.

'The paakku got over last night…must buy it.' She turned over in the bed angrily. For some time, she did not hear any movement. Then she heard him go out hurriedly.

She struggled with the tumult inside her. Venu indeed… Again and again, it was the same thought that gave rise to her

anger – how did he have the heart? Chandru immobilized…
their dear son. His disability weighed down heavily on her
heart, the sorrow indelible. Chandru…Venu…How did he
have the heart?

She heard the voices in the garden.

*Are they walking together? Is he going to take that boy to the
hotel?*

Laughter flowed as they conversed and this inflamed her.
She was filled with anger and grief. She felt an inexplicable
rage and stood up. She knew she could not bear to see them.
But she wooed the pain voluntarily.

She stood in the balcony upstairs and looked down at the
garden.

Sambasivam was talking and Gowri could see the young
man clearly. He was tall, with thick black hair and a very
pleasant smile, and looked handsome even in his simple
clothes. As Gowri looked on, her agitation swamped her and
her ears could barely hear their laughter. She was afraid she
may faint with the overpowering emotions and clutched the
balustrade with half-closed eyes.

'Amma!' Vijaya came up to her, shouting with alarm, and
held her.

Sambasivam and Venu looked up. They must have heard
her.

'Wait a minute. You said you wanted paakku.'

Was it her mother speaking? Vijaya stared. Yes, it was
Gowri who had called out to her husband, coming out of her
half-unconscious state. She released herself from Vijaya.

'Just a minute. I will bring it. Don't go.' Gowri went in.

Sambasivam was astonished. Was this the person who had fought with him upstairs with such hatred and bitterness a while ago? Was she trying to save him the embarrassment, since Venu had also seen her?

Gowri took the new packet of paakku from the shelf and went to the garden. She felt a new force energizing her.

'Here...paakku.'

Sambasivam held out his hand. But Gowri had held her hand out to Venu. She did not take her eyes off him.

'Thanks.'

The young man took the paakku from the packet in her hands and, without looking up, returned it to her.

'Namaskaram. Bye.'

The car disappeared and left an emptiness around her. But she could not erase a certain sense of fulfilment that she felt.

'Amma,' Vijaya sounded disappointed. 'In the end, by coming down you proved that women are not firm. I was happy when you showed your disapproval of Appa. I was applauding you for your self-respect. Why was it necessary to be nice to that boy?'

Gowri turned slowly. The sadness that had been there earlier was still there. It was the expression that had replaced the anger that Vijaya could not fathom.

Gowri spoke with a rush of emotions.

'Vijaya! He looks the same...identical. The face, form, everything. Today, I have seen how Chandru would have looked had he been normal. He would have been like this –

tall, impressive and happy. I have seen that Chandru today, Vijaya! God…oh god…oh god! Bless him…Now I'm not even angry with your father.'

Vijaya had felt heartbroken at a wife's distress before. Her eyes now were dazzled by the mother's ecstasy reflected in the tear-laden smile.

six

My Name is Madhavan

H E STOOD THERE, A BOY at the threshold of youth, about five-and-a-half feet tall, with a wheatish complexion bordering on fair, a half-hesitant, half-expectant face that was like a half-closed, half-open flower, cheeks toughened by a crop of acne, a pointed nose above the grin, small, fixed eyes, a high forehead and folded hands that shook a bit. He introduced himself as if to give a meaning to this form.

'My name is Madhavan.'

'Please sit down,' I said.

His feet haltingly moved two steps, feeling their way forward. I involuntarily stretched my hand to guide him, but stopped. Would he like it? Yet I looked at him with concern. With a little hesitation, but with a practised ease and a sense of pride that he had managed to move around in a strange house, he sat down on a stool and there was a big sigh – it was I who sighed, not he.

'Is the stool comfortable? If not, the chair is close by. You can sit on that.' I wanted to make him aware that he was sitting on a stool and that he should not lean back, thinking it was a chair.

'It's okay, sir. This is quite comfortable,' he, that is Madhavan, said. I had learnt his name just today.

When I first met him five months ago, he was not alone. An elderly man was with him. He was standing behind the older man, hugging a big book against his chest with his right hand. He must have just let go of the hand that had led him thus far. He was wearing crumpled but spotless, loose white shorts, and the brown shirt was dark near his armpits because of the perspiration. I thought the smile on his face was meant for me when I shouted, 'Who is that?' He was looking not at me, but at the wall! Was he squint-eyed? The next moment I saw the two glassy eyes.

'Who are you?' This time my question was not so peremptory.

'We are from an organization for sightless people.' The elderly man stopped and looked at me. He could see. He probably worked there.

'Please can you take a look at this?' Even when I took the book from him, I continued to look at the young man – sightless glass eyes, but such radiance in his face!

I looked down at the book: 'Society for the Welfare of the Sightless'. The words written in English were at the crest of the first page and at the bottom was an address in Park Town. On the left was a list of names of important members of the organization. On the right, under the heading 'Request', was written in ink, in a smudgy and shaky handwriting, a request for donation from kind benefactors to the society, which worked for the welfare of the sightless. I turned over the pages. The names of the donors and the amounts donated were recorded there.

The elderly man was telling me about the organization, but my eyes were still focused on the boy.

'Though it is only after learning skills like cane work, carpentry, basket-weaving, etc. from the training school on Poonamallee High Road that they come to us, we nurture and develop their skills by giving them training. We keep writing to other organizations, asking them to reserve some posts for the visually challenged. Many get jobs and some even get married.'

The sightless. In the book, the words used were 'the sightless'. For some reason, this sounded more humane than 'the blind'. I felt that the older man's complete avoidance of the word 'blind' was a meaningful omission. The words 'sightless', 'speech disabled' and 'hearing disabled' did not denote contempt, unlike the words 'blind', 'deaf' and 'dumb' They did not express scorn or scathing contempt; instead, they seemed to say 'accept your unfortunate friends'.

'We...approach...individuals...like this just like...we receive donations from the rich people and the government.'

I looked at the amounts written down on the brown, dog-eared pages, which had a grimy smell – 50 paise, 5 rupees, 1 rupee, 2 rupees... One rupee was the amount that occurred the most frequently. After giving the book back to the senior man, I pulled out a rupee from the wallet in my shirt pocket.

'Thanks, sir.'

The younger man followed suit and also gestured his thanks, his smile again directed at the wall.

After that, they started coming every month. And I gave them a rupee every month. I was eager to get to know the young man. But the older man's presence stopped me. When both of them said farewell, I felt like dragging him by his folded hands and bringing him in.

'Who are you? What is the truth hidden in that "you"? Which is this other world whose leader you are? Which is the inner space that you seem to rule? Will you not reveal to me that inner you? Will you not grant me that vision?' My heart beat hard as I yearned to plead with him for answers.

'See you,' was all I would say.

He was fragile, like a book that one had to open gently and carefully, by blowing on it. How do I approach him?

The opportunity came one day. Looking at him, I gave the rupee to the older man. From inside the house, the clatter of the typewriter could be heard. 'Tat tat tat tat tat.'

His face brightened up at once. 'Is it a typewriter, sir?'

'Yes.'

'Do you have one? Do you type?'

'I don't. The machine belongs to my sister's son. He has gone out of town for some training. He has left it with me till he comes back. If my neighbours want something to be typed urgently, they come and type it here. The girl next door asked me this morning if she could type an article for her college magazine. She is here.'

He was silent for a while. His face expressed joy and his head was bent to one side as he listened intently.

'Tat tat tat tat tat tat tatat tatat tatat tatat.'

'I think she has made some mistake. That is why she is scoring it out.' It was only when he said that that I noticed how the keys sounded different from the way they had the last time. I looked at him in surprise.

'Do you know how to type? Do they teach you that too?'

'No, sir. There are separate Braille machines for that. We don't have them. He had learnt to type even before, …before he lost his vision.' The older man explained.

'Lost his…'

'I was interested in that, though I was doing odd jobs,' he intervened and picked up the trail. 'My factory owner was a good man. He arranged for me to learn free of cost at an institute run by his friend. He even told me I would get a good job afterwards. I learnt typing for two years at that institute. I liked it very much.' His fingers danced away as if they were typing.

'At first, I would furtively look at the letters and type, and the teacher would yell at me. He would cover the keys with a piece of cloth and ask me to type, or tell me to type with my eyes closed…' He stopped for a minute, as if he was staring at the last two words, and then burst out laughing.

I turned away, forgetting that he could not see the sorrow flooding my face.

Factory…what kind of factory? Was it a factory accident that had bli…that had robbed him of his sight? There may be a thousand reasons – how did it matter? He may have become incapable of working or maybe the owner had died and the factory had closed – how did it matter? The fact of the matter was that he was bereft of all support. He was still lost in thought.

'So even now, you can type on ordinary machines, not necessarily Braille, no?' I asked him eagerly.

'Oh, yes! It is just a touch system. All I need to do is to position my fingers right when I start.'

I did some quick thinking. My wife had caught the literary bug from the girl next door. She had written a pile of stories full of romance and pathos, to be sent to some monthly journals. After reading them, I had sternly resisted the idea of getting them typed, but I now found a use for them.

'My wife writes stories. If someone reads aloud, can you type them? They are in English. I will pay at the usual rate. You can come when it's convenient and I will accompany you back to the hostel.'

His face lit up like ten thousand lamps. His body shook as if the dance of the fingers vibrated through it. His wide grin revealed his gums. The smile on his raised face was not for me, but directed elsewhere.

'Yes sir, I'll come sir. What is your machine, sir? Is it Remington portable? I am used to that. Even if it is upstairs, I can manage by climbing slowly. If I do it carefully for two days, I'll get used to it.'

That's how this started. The hostel permitted him to come. After all, this was another source of income for him. Then a day was fixed and the elderly man brought him home. He stood in excited anticipation. It was then that I asked him, as a step towards forging familiarity and closeness, 'What is your name?'

He told me. I realized that the name 'Madhavan' stood for this boy and his eagerness, his liveliness, his young age, which was half of mine, and his misfortune and the smile in the midst of it.

He sat on the stool for merely two seconds.

'Where is the machine, sir?'

I took him to his seat. He leant on the table and stroked and touched the machine with both hands. Then he bent and rested his face on it, and a smile spilled from his lips.

Then he was not there; he was somewhere else. Where? At the factory? Or at the typewriting institute? In those days, eyes meant vision. He could see then – a world that had colour, shapes. He saw people and their forms. He could look at both sides and dart his glance across the road before the distant bus came close… The black eyes slyly looked at the board while typing with dexterity…tat tattatat tattatat. The voice that asked him to type with his eyes closed belonged to a face which had a stern expression. He could look at him with a mischievous smile. He could look at the machine and stop typing before the bell rang to indicate that he had reached the edge of the paper. And then? And what else? What other sights were locked inside the glass eyes?

71

He was not there and I could not follow him…because I can see.

He looked up and slowly ran his fingers over the machine.

'Is this small machine a Remington?'

'No. Hermes.'

'I must get used to it. Can you give me a sheet of paper?'

With ease and just by touch, he fixed the paper in the middle of the cylinder. His fingers measured the space and were then ready on the keys.

'A-S-D-F-G-F'

His face focused inward, the letters came out as though they were religious chants.

After the middle row, he went to the second row from the top.

'Q-W-E-R-T-R'

I kept watching his face. I had called my wife to introduce him to her. She came and stood there looking him up and down, with the manuscript in her hands.

The fingers of his right hand, starting from the little finger, were now on the bottom row, moving over the keys as if counting them.

'Full stop, comma, M-N-B – I haven't forgotten at all, sir! I remember everything! Shall I now check by typing the alphabet – A-B-C-D-E-F-G?'

The fingers flew over the keys. I looked at my wife, full of appreciation for him. My mother stood behind my wife and the way she looked at him, I could sense that for her it was like a circus trick.

'V-W-X-Y-Z-full stop. Sir, I have come to the end. Will you please check if it is correct?'

I took a look at the sheet of paper.

'Excellent! Absolutely correct.'

Pride and joy flashed on his face.

'Nothing surprising. I have not forgotten anything. But it is a different machine, …some keys may be in a different place…for example…' The index finger jabbed a key on the top row. 'In that machine this was a hyphen…Is it so here too?'

Emotion choked me, but I steadied myself, looking at his cheerful face.

'Why are you silent, sir? Are you wondering because there are two marks on the same key? Tell me what is at the bottom.'

'This is not a hyphen.'

'See? There may be such minor variations. Just tell me what is on the top row in order, and I will memorize it. The numbers will be in the same places. Tell me the other marks. Even if you do not understand, it does not matter – I will.'

He was in his domain and assurance, self-confidence and pride came naturally. This was the real him. It exhilarated me as I called out the keys, and as I did so, he touched them to commit to memory. Then to practise, he typed a few sentences.

'Is it correct, sir?'

I bent down.

'In one place it is "i" instead of "e".'

He typed the sentence again.

'Now?'

'Correct.'

'I'm ready.'

I called my wife and introduced them. He said 'vanakkam' to her.

Then he briskly started the work.

'Ma'am, just tell me when I come to the end of the sheet and I will insert a fresh one. Will you now give me the sheets of paper for typing? As soon as I insert one, we can start. Double-spacing, no? One plus one or two...Oh, sorry! How many copies do you need? Have you bought carbon paper?' He continued to speak excitedly, the sightless one. I looked on at him with a smile. My wife did not answer.

It was my mother who spoke. 'Great! The blind boy is so clever! He can even type!'

He straightened up. Was his complexion wheatish and almost fair? No. This was just white. The blood had drained out of his face. Just white. The exuberance, liveliness, human dignity and unyielding self-confidence had all gone...he had died.

The sightless one slowly rose from the chair.

'Sir, take me up to the gate, will you? After that, I will go by myself, I'm used to it.'

I stared at my mother's face just once. Without a word, I held his hand and started walking. What right had I to ask him to stay or even talk to him? He would never come here again.

He reached the doorstep. Then he looked in the direction from which my mother's voice had come. He turned his face.

'My name is not "blind boy".' He took four steps beyond the door and said in a tired voice: 'My name is Madhavan.'

I crossed the collapsible gate and took him outside.

seven

An Old Movie

L OOKING AT THAT HOUSE FROM THE OUTSIDE, no one would guess it consisted of four residential units. But it did.

There were two rooms eight square feet each, and a kitchen that looked as if it was attached as an afterthought. This was one 'portion'. The ground floor had two portions, and the first floor two. The house owner and his wife occupied one portion of the ground floor.

At the rear of the building were two bathrooms and two toilets. It should not be concluded that each of these pairs of rooms was meant to benefit two families. The owner had exclusive rights over one bathroom–toilet pair. The other pair had to be shared by the other three families. The house rent was 400 rupees and the electricity charges 50 rupees; the water charges another 50 rupees. The tenants could sit in the front porch and enjoy the fresh air – that came for free.

If the water pump broke down, it would be fixed at the cost of the family that was held responsible for the breakdown. If anyone complained that the roof leaked or that the floor had chipped, they were free to leave the place and look for alternative accommodation. The owner had no objection. A long queue of people were waiting to occupy any portion, willing to pay seven hundred or eight hundred. It was the owner, out of pity for his tenants, who did not drive them away. Who but an idiot would let out a portion in Purasaivakkam in Chennai for a measly 400 rupees?

Venkatachalam, the owner, had three such houses in Chennai. Without stirring from his place, he lived in comfort with the rental income. No one had a clue what he did in his younger days, how he became the owner of four houses. His two sons were well placed, working in north India. But Venkatachalam had no wish to live with them. At sixty, he was happy to lord it over the people in his own house, sitting in comfort, bossing over his wife, stroking his salt-and-pepper moustache, and being a nightmare to his tenants. Could this pleasure have been matched if he had been under his sons' control, even if he were offered feasts every day?

The portion on the right on the first floor was occupied by a couple between thirty and thirty-five years of age. Rajan and Valarmathi had two daughters, eight and six years old – their only heirs and the light of their lives. Both husband and wife were employed in small companies. The income was not much; it was an ordinary middle-class existence, with the family managing between debts and dreams. From the time they woke up till they flopped down to sleep, it was an incessant grind – housework, office stress, worries of rearing the children, and the unending problems of life. Unknown to them, their lives were slipping through their fingers.

The portion on the left on the first floor was occupied by an elderly single woman – Nagalakshmi. She would not be less than sixty-five. Maybe she could even have been described as a burnished gold statue when she was young? Now, time had left its imprint on her face and body. Like the lovely magizham flowers which are fragrant even after they have faded, the elegant lovely face, with wide deep eyes and beautiful lips held a lingering beauty.

It was said that she had been affluent once. Maybe her husband had left her or maybe she had never married. She wore red kumkum on her forehead, but there was no tali around her neck. She must have been betrayed by a man she had loved and trusted. Maybe he had cheated on her and made off with her wealth. All this was just idle speculation by the neighbours. She never opened up and shared her personal life with anyone. It seemed her sister's son had sold what remained with her, and supplemented it with his own contribution and invested it wisely for her. That's how she was able to live here with some dignity. This information she had volunteered herself.

The right portion on the ground floor was occupied by Sivanesan – a retired school teacher, his wife Neelamani and daughter Thamarai. Thamarai was twenty-eight. As soon as she got her BA degree, she started working as a typist in her father's school. She had two brothers, but they went away soon after they got married. Thamarai could not get married because her father was not well off and her brothers did not care. Her parents fretted sadly, in silence.

But Thamarai was not sad. She was by nature an optimist. She was not self-pitying and was a gregarious person who made friends with everyone. On days when her brothers wanted to go out with their wives, they would leave their children with her.

'Thamarai, can you take care of them? You are so fond of children and they dote on their Athai. We will pick them up on our way home.'

This would anger her parents, but not Thamarai. She played with the children, fed them and put them to sleep. Even if this meant that she could not fully watch her favourite Tamil movie on TV, it did not bother her.

Once she told her despondent parents, 'Please think that my brothers are daughters who have left you after marriage, and I am the son who will always be with you and take care of you.'

Was this any comfort? But she said it in all sincerity, and with grace.

It was not just her brothers' children; she was willing to look after the children of Valarmathi, the woman upstairs, too. Valarmathi and Rajan came home from work late on some days and the children had to be fed as soon as they returned from school. Valarmathi had entrusted this responsibility only to Nagalakshmi, who lived in the other portion upstairs.

'Why do you trouble Paatti? I'll do it.' When Thamarai offered to help, Valarmathi would cut her short with a glare.

'No need.'

Valarmathi did not like the friendly familiarity with which Thamarai spoke to everyone, including Rajan.

'The poor, innocent girl,' Rajan would intervene.

'Stop it. Whatever it is, shouldn't a girl remember she has to behave with propriety when talking to a man?'

Valarmathi suspected that Thamarai, a frustrated spinster, was looking to ensnare her husband. She was convinced that her offer to help with the children was motivated by the intention to get close to Rajan.

Nagalakshmi was not very enthusiastic about babysitting. It was not that she was unhelpful at heart. But those brats… would they eat their snacks and be quiet?

'Paatti, Paatti!' they screamed. They messed up her things, jumped on her bed, crumpled her folded clothes…

'Is this your petticoat, Paatti? Amma's is longer.'

Then trooping into the kitchen, trying to turn the gas on and taking off the lids of her vessels to see what was for dinner…Appappa…creatures from Kishkinda…real monkeys of the Ramayana.

'Paatti, please tell us a story.'

'Paatti…paatti. I am no paatti to anyone. I do not know these Aesop's stories and Panchatantra tales…Just go…'

'Tell us a story you know.'

'Mmm…a movie story?'

'Yes, yes, we love cinema stories…*Doom doom…En*

machaan kanni vechaan… Just noise and chaos.'

'Once upon a time, there was a king. He had a beautiful daughter…'

Nagalakshmi would drown in the story. Her eyes would soften and a strange radiance would light them up.

'Then…'

When the story ended, they would clap with joy.

'One more story, Paatti.'

'No no, I'm going to lie down. My knees hurt. Please go to your room and do your homework. When your Appa and Amma come home, they will spank you if you are sitting with me, listening to stories.'

Nagalakshmi would lie down on her side, a crumpled clothes heap, and close her eyes with a sigh.

Not wanting to do their homework, the kids would go down and play in the central hall.

'Hey, hey! What's this noise? Go up quietly to Nagu Paatti's room, or I'll kill you!' This was Venkatachalam's threat.

'It was Paatti who asked us to go down,' they replied with trepidation.

'Only a married woman with children would know how special they are. Come to me, my dears. Please keep quiet, Aiya does not like noise,' said Venkatachalam's wife, Bhagyaththammaal.

'Is it enough to have children? I too have two sons – good-for-nothing fellows – who couldn't care less about their parents or their sister… Selfish devils. I'd rather have been childless.' This was Neelamani's moan.

'Neela, keep quiet. It's our fate.' Sivanesan would admonish her.

'If Valarmathi Akka and Rajan Anna agree, I will happily babysit their children, whenever I am at home.' This was Thamarai.

If by chance, Valarmathi happened to return from office and heard this, she would chase the children upstairs.

'People with a poor character need not take care of my kids. (Rajan Anna, indeed! Who is she trying to fool?) Hey Anu, Subha, run upstairs. If I see you with such people again, I'll break your feet.'

'People who comment on others must first teach their kids to behave properly in others' houses,' Nagalakshmi, standing at the top of the stairs, would put in her bit at the right moment.

Exchanging looks that could kill each other, the residents would disappear into their respective portions.

But there was one time when all these squabbles melted away and everyone gathered together in complete amity. That was on Sunday evenings when Tamil movies were telecast.

The TV sat imperiously on a table under the fluorescent light against the blue wall in the central hall. The kind of respect it received was such that one could only say that it sat imperiously. Venkatachalam stopped short of worshipping it. He had done even that when the Ramayana serial was being telecast. So what if he did not understand Hindi? Rama is Rama in any language, isn't he? On the day that Seetha Parinayam, Paduka Pattabhishekam and Rama Pattabhishekam were shown, he had garlanded the TV and performed the ritual of prayer with a lighted lamp and flowers.[2]

Every day he would take off the TV cover and wipe it carefully till it shone, and then put it back on. Every week, he washed the cover himself with Ariel detergent. On days when the cover was off, he would place a new curio on the TV and rejoice in that.

No one could touch the TV, and that included his wife. He would adjust the colour and brightness, and the remote control was always with him. When the programme ended, it was he who switched off the TV. He had chosen to live on the ground floor only to prevent others from operating the TV. There were times when Bhagyaththammal got very irritated and grumbled to Neelamani out of his earshot.

'The TV is his second wife.'

If he came along with his coffee and reclined comfortably on one of the two sofas that was placed at the right distance, it indicated that he was generously permitting the others to join him. One by one, the others would troop in and sit on the chairs.

'At least for some time, we forget our worries, no?' This was Nilamani's frequent excuse.

'Sometimes there are good messages, especially if it is an old movie.'

'Nowadays, films have too much violence or women-centred obscenity. Impossible to watch them. But that's how the world is,' Bhagyaththammal would say with a sigh, but she would unfailingly sit on the second sofa like the royal consort.

Nagalakshmi would hurry downstairs quietly, her face and eyes all intent, holding her knees and taking one step at a time.

Valarmathi and Rajan too would watch the movies on the Sundays when they did not go elsewhere.

'Tamil movies are rotten,' Rajan would comment, but he too would watch the film because how can one gauge the degree of rottenness without seeing it?

Valarmathi liked Tamil movies. When young modern women raved about American movies and Italian movies, she felt embarrassed to admit that she liked Tamil movies. She would sit down, taking care to explain that she was watching the movie only because she was bored. An added attraction was that this entertainment came for free. *After all, it is brought directly to our homes. Are we spending even a paisa on it or what?*

Of course, she could not fully enjoy the movie if her husband and children were with her. She had to make sure that Thamarai was nowhere around. She had to look out in case Thamarai made any signals to Rajan. She had to see if he (after all, he is a man, no?) was, in fact, looking only at the screen and nowhere else. She had to quieten down the children when they embarrassed her by asking questions about the Whisper sanitary napkins ad.

Thamarai would offer no such explanation. If her brothers had left their children with her, she would keep them near her. If she did not like the movie, she would leave in the middle. During the children's meal times or bedtime, she went in. If she was not babysitting and the movie was good, she watched the whole movie.

Apart from the residents, the maid, who came early in the morning and finished her work in all four portions in just two hours, watched the movies, sitting on the floor. Venkatachalam permitted this reluctantly; he had no option. If he did not let her watch, she would stop working. There was no recent movie that she had not watched. Her knowledge was unparalleled. Who acted with whom, who was the second heroine – Janusri or Banusri – she had the answers at her command.

If it was an old movie, the seniors were thrilled. They rejoiced in watching Tyagaraja Bhagavatar, P.U. Chinnappa, Kannaambaa, Rajakumari Anjali Devi… – the matinee idols of their era.

'What a bore…if they sit down they sing; if they get up also there is a song,' Rajan grumbled.

Nagalakshmi butted in, 'How can you say that? Those movies had a story value. Not like today's movies, of which you can make neither head nor tail.' Whatever her opinion, Nagalakshmi watched all the movies from beginning to end.

'Paatti loves movies. She will be watching even after "The End" is shown,' Venkatachalam teased her.

'Am I a paatti to you, too?' Sharp words from the fine lips.

'What is this? He is just teasing you…' Valarmathi would pacify her, keen on averting a misunderstanding. If Venkatachalam got upset halfway through the film, he would switch off the TV and go away.

But today he was not likely to do that. It was a 45-year-old movie. He had probably seen it for the first time when he was a schoolboy.

Bhagyaththammal, Nagalakshmi, Sivanesan and Neelamani were all engrossed in the movie. 'This has a very moving story. I have seen it,' Sivanesan had certified in advance.

Nagalakshmi did not say anything. She sat on a chair very close to the TV and was lost in the movie.

A Raja–Rani story. The Raja and Rani were good people. They had an only child, the princess Chandravadani. The wicked army chief, Kroora Varman, plotted to capture the throne and marry her. The handsome and brave prince of the neighbouring kingdom, Rajasimhan, foiled the plot, saved the king and queen, and married the princess (without revealing himself until the end). Mayavaram Kamalanathan, who acted as the prince, and G. Tilottama, who played the princess, were the leading stars of those days.

During the scene of the swayamvaram, in which many princes competed for the princess' hand, Neelamani looked at her daughter sadly.

'Hmm, how many men came on their own to marry a girl in those days.'

'Even today they would, if she were a king's daughter,' said Sivanesan.

'A king's daughter does not remain a king's daughter forever,' Nagalakshmi said, without taking her eyes off the screen.

'Ssh, don't chatter...just watch.' Venkatachalam's reprimand was followed by silence.

Princess Chandravadani stood in the balcony, looking up, and sang a song in raga Kalyani. She asked the moon why her heart tossed restlessly ever since she saw the young man who lived in the forest.

The tired children had fallen asleep near their mother's feet.

'Paatti, don't sit so close to the TV. Bad for your eyes,' Rajan said, and then laughed. 'Looks like you will go and sit inside the TV box.'

Indeed, Nagalakshmi was looking at Chandravadani as though she would swallow her in one piece.

'What a film-crazy person she is!' Thamarai thought as she stood up. The movie was boring. Neither the brothers, nor their children had come. She was free to go to sleep.

She had taken two steps when a close-up of G. Tilottama's face appeared on the TV screen. Something struck her sharply. Her feet halted and she peered closely at the face. A very elegant oval face, deep eyes and thin lips throbbing with emotion.

She turned towards Nagalakshmi. The aged eyes watching the screen were slightly wet. In a moment, the screen of Time swung and fell off her face as it appeared totally transformed.

Thamarai held her breath and stared transfixed.

eight

The Blue Lotus Drooped

IT WAS STILL HOT, THOUGH it was evening. He was wiping his perspiring face all the time with the towel on his shoulder as he walked. Next to him was his wife.

So many different posters were stuck on the roadside walls – cinema posters, political advertisements!

They were walking on the bridge from Adyar. The traffic going in opposite directions was divided by a median, and from the pedestrian path they could see the river and the Adyar palace.

Sharma's worry-filled heart was tempered by literary fragrance. Epics, poetry and knowledge…why did people not consider Sanskrit literature the literature of knowledge? Wasn't it surprising that they eschewed something that appealed to the head and heart? Did rationalism mean that knowledge should be erased?

'No one paused even for a moment to think of how

beautiful Sanskrit is, you see!'

Karpagam did not answer.

'Why hate a language?' Sharma asked. Karpagam paid no heed; for her the subject was worn thin by now.

She hazily remembered his initial outburst: 'What? Removing Sanskrit totally from the curriculum?' and the intensity with which he wept for the language, like a mother for her child.

'The matter is now closed; why weep?' she had tried to console him. She stopped when she saw that he had shut the door to such consolation. She was also conscious that she could never fully comprehend this loss, this pain of his. As far as she was concerned, this language was a source of income for her husband. What could she say to him, a person for whom it was beauty, love, knowledge, life; in fact, a many-splendoured thing? Her silence as she witnessed his rejection of the government's offer to relocate him as a librarian or in some other post was testimony to her loyalty to him.

'Karpagam, Sanskrit is not this man's or that man's property. You know that, right? It is our country's wealth, it is our country's pride, it is our culture, and it is Indianness…if you ask me, I would say that having at least a smattering of Sanskrit knowledge is the mark of an Indian.'

'My legs hurt.'

'Do you know that universities abroad teach Sanskrit? Can we neglect it here?'

'We have been walking for a long time…Shall we sit somewhere?'

'How can you say that the value of and love for Tamil will get diminished because one studies Sanskrit?'

'I can't walk any more. Please, let's take a bus.'

Rajagopala Sharma turned to look at his wife. How tired she looked! Her hair was dishevelled, she was panting a little. Sweat had smudged the dot of kumkum on her forehead. He felt sorry for her. Poor Karpagam! She had to face hardships for having committed the sin of marrying him. Being reduced to poverty after stubbornly rejecting the offer of librarianship may give him moral satisfaction. Valmiki, Kalidasa, Bhasa and Bhartrihari – the greats of Sanskrit literature – may appear in his dreams and sweeten the poverty. But what about her?

'You want to go by bus?'

He hesitated as he still felt the humiliation they had faced the last time they had tried to board a bus. He in his dhoti, worn the traditional way, with his hair tied in a knot and vibhuti (sacred ash) on his forehead, and she in her nine-yard sari had run towards the bus. Just as they were about to board it, the conductor had deliberately and gleefully blown the whistle. Didn't he feel compassion for them at least on account of their age? The bus did stop…but ten feet away.

'Sorry sir, I did not notice you. Get in Maamiii…,' the conductor had drawled insolently and some of the passengers had rewarded him with appreciative laughter.

Mercifully, nothing of the sort happened when they got in this time.

Sharma read a couplet from Thiruvalluvar's *Tirukkural* written on the wall of the bus.

'I have inherited the wealth of both Valluvar and Valmiki. Neither can be forced on me or taken away from me,' Sharma wanted to shout.

He was a Tamilian and he loved Tamil. Was he obliged to sacrifice Sanskrit to prove his love for Tamil? Would Tamil die if Sanskrit was taught in government schools?

He would, of course, voice his objection. His devotion to Sanskrit, his love of the language and the way his pulse throbbed for it could not be channelled elsewhere.

Was he not even now headed to a friend's house in Mylapore for this very reason? He had been invited to discuss certain verses of Valmiki's Ramayana before a select audience. He would share with them the exquisite sweetness of the language by reciting and explaining the verses. The happiness he felt needed no explanation. Just as the cuckoo that was Valmiki sang the name of Rama, he too would trill with joy. That was all.

Karpagam's face drooped. They had not eaten well for the last few days. He was to blame. How could he refuse to accept the job that was offered when another life depended on him?

To divert his mind from this feeling of guilt, he started reciting a Sanskrit verse.

In the jewelled hall King Rama was seated, like a blue lotus. He was seated there surrounded by his wife, Seetha, his brothers and those who were like his brothers, Hanuman, Angada and Jambavan.

Adisankara's imagination was indeed beautiful and he had rightly chosen the simile of a blue lotus which so aptly and eloquently described the epic beauty of the language. Epic beauty was the right term, according to Sharma. It was not merely a matter of the ritualistic chanting of verses, or ancient tales about divine beings or descriptive verses about god. What he saw in it was lyrical beauty, lyrical excellence.

He sat melting in that beauty. The sky darkened, portending rain.

They got off at the Tank Stop. The radiance with which Sanskrit, in all its glory sat in his heart remained undisturbed. As he entered the friend's house, he was welcomed with the words, 'Today, Neela...' Sharma was still immersed in his own thoughts. 'Yes, the Neelakantam, the blue-throated Siva, Neela tamarai, the blue lotus...So it means that beauty stands distilled as blue, right?'

'What?'

Sharma turned red with embarrassment.

'Obviously you have been thinking of something...and that spilt out as words.' The friend smiled.

'True, and I became a gopika.'

'Meaning?'

'What do you do with this author, Lilasukar, who steals your heart with his poetry on Krishna's exploits? He writes that the gopika goes around selling curds, butter, etc., and instead of shouting "Curds!", she shouts what is in her heart – Krishna by his various names, "Govinda, Damodara, Madhava".'

'So her business would have gone "Govinda" – kaput!' Karpagam burst out.

Sharma fell silent.

'What were you about to say?'

'Nothing…You know our Neelakanta Rao, the owner of "Radha transport", don't you? It seems his daughter is very interested in Sanskrit slokas. She wants to come this evening. So he is bringing her along too.'

There were only a select few in the room. The host's wife served pieces of sugared melon and some buttermilk. Karpagam felt a little refreshed.

Neelakanta Rao introduced his daughter to Sharma.

'Radha loves Sanskrit. I have requested a tutor to teach her at home. She is an earnest learner.'

'I'm glad. What are you reading now…Magha or Megha or something else?'

'Mr Sharma, that child will not understand your code words,' one of the guests intervened. He explained, 'Radha, he wants to know if you are reading any of Magha's works or Kalidasa's *Megha Sandesham* or something else.'

'I have not come that far, Mama. I have started to learn only recently.'

'She is engaged to be married. I hope that family encourages her interest,' said her father, affection and worry apparent in his voice. The girl felt shy and bent her head.

Sharma was fired with enthusiasm. 'Look at her! Blushing on hearing the mention of her marriage…even Parvathi…'

'Which Parvathi?'

'How many Parvathis are there? The Seven Sages came to her father, Himavan, to ask for her hand on behalf of Shiva.

Parvathi stood next to her father, her head bent, counting the petals of a lotus that she held in her hand. What imagery! They say Kalidasa reigns supreme in similes. But here it is another poetic grace that comes through!'

'What grace? Curd rice?' Karpagam's soft explosion was heard by all.

They were all discomfited. But not Rajagopala Sharma!

'Exactly!' He punched the air with his finger, his face shining. 'Curd rice it is. The song says curds made of buffalo's milk. But how he describes the whiteness of the curds! He compares it to the whiteness of the autumn moon. Bhojan understood at once who the poet was. Who else could have written this? Not for nothing is Kalidasa lauded.'

The host who had invited him wondered when Sharma would stop rambling and come to the subject. His patience began to wear thin.

'Shall we start Valmiki?' someone asked.

'Sure.'

Sharma was seated silently in the centre. His eyes were focused inward. It was as if he was extending his hand in invitation to Valmiki for him to come and bless his words.

Some of the guests had brought their copies of the Ramayana. Sharma did not need that aid. Sanskrit literature was there in his heart and his very breath. He dived into the treasure of the Ramayana for the gems and began to speak. He drew everyone into his recitation. He plunged them into an ideal, golden dream of a wonderful time from a bygone era, and their breath was arrested with ecstasy.

'...magnificent like the ocean, unshakeable like the Himalayas, when angry he was like the epochal fire, when patient he was like the earth.'

The clock ticked 'Ram Ram Ram.' The story unfolded as a bridge between the listeners' ears and the speaker's voice.

Sharma's heart dissolved in the thrill and sweetness of his experience. The discourse came to an end, but he remained in that trance. The sweetness receded and he opened his eyes.

What was this? From where had this crowd come? There had been only seven or eight in the beginning...Now the hall was full and overflowing into the passage...

His heart leapt with joy. Did people like Sanskrit so much? Valmiki, sir, you are a wizard...Who can destroy this language?

The crowd got up with a rustle.

'Excellent religious discourse!'

'But there was no board outside indicating that there is a discourse today...'

'No mention even in "Today's engagements" in the newspapers.'

'It is our good fortune. We heard something good.'

'What else? It is not easy to come by an opportunity to listen to a talk on the divine.'

The host was thrilled.

'We are proud that so many of you came and listened. Blessed is the one who spoke, and equally blessed are the ones who gathered to hear him'.

'We listened to Rama's story and our sins were washed

away.' Saying this, one stretched out his hand with a contribution and he was followed by many.

'I thought you would pass the contribution plate around. Maybe you forgot,' an old voice added.

The coins fell on the plate with a clatter.

'Why didn't we think of this earlier? What if it is not taught in schools and colleges? Sanskrit will always be welcome here. There will always be a crowd for such religious discourses. One can earn a lot if it is pursued as a profession. Sharma, don't worry at all. We totally forgot how popular these discourses are. It is now the renaissance of devotion.'

Sharma sat still and silent like a statue. He could not come out of the shock. The eyes were still fixed, and all that the eyes saw was a blue lotus drooping sadly.

'Sharma, Sanskrit will be the source of your livelihood, as you wished. You will beat all other religious speakers with your expertise.'

Sharma did not look up.

'It is rare to find people like you. Amazing how Sanskrit pours out of you like a torrent. Remarkable! Even though I could not understand anything, I was stunned,' said another.

'Nurturing devotion like this is a good deed,' yet another voice sounded.

Sharma started laughing. The coins were heaped on the plate. He looked at it and laughed uncontrollably.

'Karpagam, I came here to share my appreciation of poetic aesthetics. Not to give a discourse. But do you see they have collected contributions? Divine blessings, it seems. Everyone heard the Ramayana, no one listened to the poetry.'

He somehow managed to say this and laughed again. There were tears in his eyes. Was he laughing or crying? It was hard to say.

'Upanyasakarval, the religious speaker sir...' a slightly puzzled man began.

Sharma lifted his hand to halt him. The tears and the laughter had dried up in an instant.

'I am not a religious speaker. I am a librarian.' He turned to his wife.

'I will accept that job, Karpagam.'

Karpagam kept silent with relief.

nine

The Dancing Ganesha

'Do you know your name?'
The little girl laughed.

'Ayye! As if I won't know.'

'Then tell me.'

'I've told you before.'

'Tell me again.'

'Meeeenalochaneee.'

Along with her name she too stretched to her full majestic five-year-old height.

'No, that is not your name.'

'Hmm?'

'Your name is not Meenalochani.'

'It is.'

'No.'

'Then what is my name?'

'Suthanthira (freedom).'

Nandu uttered the name softly, as though reciting an incantation in the same breath.

'Your name is Suthanthira.'

The little face frowned.

'No, my name is Meenalochani. I don't like the other name, nor do I like you.'

The voice was filled with tears. She seemed to be shocked at the rejection of her name, as if her identity had been denied. It was too heavy a burden for a child to be riddled with the question, 'Who am I?'

Nandu stopped the child from going away by holding her hand.

'Don't get angry. You're Meenalochani to everyone and to yourself. But to me you are Suthanthira. Since I like you very much, I have given you a pet name. Now you have two names – Meenalochani and Suthanthira.'

Suthanthira laughed joyously on receiving this sudden windfall.

When she saw the little girl seated casually with a regal air on a bundle of dirty clothes on the cart drawn by the old man, Nandu felt that the name 'Suthanthira' was inscribed on her feet. She was walking along Thana Street with the bag of vegetables in one hand and Paappa her little son in the other…She felt that the walk to the market would be an outing in the fresh air for him, and would be of help to her mother too. It was then that she saw Suthanthira, as though she were a vision. The descending rays of the sun falling on the child burnished her with a golden glow by sheer chance.

It looked like the halo that adorns a god. The child was the goddess of freedom, seated at a height untouched by this world's sorrows.

Child, freedom…two words with the same meaning.

Four days later, the old man, followed by his granddaughter, had come home. He had delivered the laundered clothes and picked up the clothes to be washed. Nandu's surprise dissolved in joy when she saw them. While he was sorting out the clothes inside, the girl sat outside on the front steps, singing to herself. The yellow frock shone brightly against her dark skin. Her curly hair was plaited and fastened with a violet clip on the top. There must be a loving mother or grandmother at home. Nandu went with her child and sat next to her, and extended a friendly smile.

'What is your name, my dear?'

The little girl looked her up and down and turned her head away smartly.

'Why don't you reply?'

No reply.

'Do you know my name? It is Nandini.'

Nandu's ruse worked. The girl turned her head towards Nandu and, not to be beaten in this name game, said, 'My name is Meenalochani.' Then she raised her eyebrows. 'Who are you? I have never seen you before.'

'You know the Amma and Aiya of this house?'

'Mmm.'

'I am their daughter.'

'Chinnamma alone is their daughter.'

'I am their older daughter. I have come from Bangalore. This is my son.'

Meenalochani lowered her eyes to look at the son.

'What is your name?'

'He won't talk.'

'Doesn't he know how to speak? He is soooo big. Then you tell me his name.'

'Paappa (child).'

'Ayye! It is obvious he's a child. I'm asking his name.'

'His name is Paappa too.'

How she longed for the day when he would come and she could call him Madanagopal and hear him say 'Amma' and come running to hug her.

Paappa sat next to her in the same position as she had placed him. She had her arm around him to keep him from falling. He had the physical growth of a two-year old but his fixed eyes were lifeless. She wiped the saliva that dribbled from his mouth with a towel.

She could hear voices from inside the house.

'Veshti.'

'Two'

'Blouse.'

'Four.'

'Is the new silk blouse there? The blue one with checks?'

'It is here, Amma.'

'Okay. Churidar?'

'Shall we be friends?' Nandu asked the girl.

It was only after the friendship was affirmed that she shared the secret.

'Your name is Suthanthira.'

'These days, which washerman comes home to collect the clothes? This man is an old-timer and also lives in Purasaivaakkam…my good fortune,' Amma said, as she came to the front room after setting the cooker on the stove.

Nandu stood looking at the small Ganesha statuette in sandstone, with a sandalwood-coloured enamel coating, which stood on the TV. She was not impressed by Ganesha's crown or his four hands or the left foot that rested on the ground. It was the right foot that captivated her; turned sideways, with the heel raised and the toes alone touching the ground. The artist had captured Ganesha in a moment of that dance movement. The next moment that foot would rest on the ground and the left foot would be raised, with just the toes on the ground. This foot after that…thakkita tharikita… the toes not quite resting on the ground. Joy and abandon had fully permeated the movement.

'Otherwise I would have to run to the laundry on the days that the maid does not turn up for work.'

'Why? Can't Appa or Kala go?'

'Kala, indeed…She has time just for her romance. And your father – fat chance of him going to the laundry. He will shout the house down, asking me if he is a washerman. Don't you know his attitude when it comes to housework?'

Nandu knew about not just her father's attitude…she

knew about Paappa's father's attitude too.

'Muthu, I'm very tired. I will lie down for some more time. Can you heat the milk, please? I will come and make my coffee,' she had asked him one morning after a bout of fever.

'No chance. Housework is your duty.'

'The house is yours too.'

'A discourse on feminism?'

'If I ask for human kindness, is it feminism?'

'Are you saying I am a beast?'

This was just a sample. She had been shocked to encounter the many ugly things in her five years of married life. It was meant to be a bond tied by trust. She had dreamt that it would bring with it a lifelong friendship. Everything ended with the question, 'Was this the man I married?'

Then those words came as the final nail.

'Nandu, tomorrow evening I have invited a very important person and his wife for tea. He is a business acquaintance. It is an honour that he has accepted my invitation. The food must be really special. As his wife is coming, you must join us. Don't appear before them with this wonderful thing you have given birth to. It must not show its face while they are here.'

She felt as if the crown of heartlessness had cracked and fallen on her head.

Should she live with him even after this?

This was the only thought on her mind ever since she had come to her parents' house with her son.

Amma was horrified.

'What is this thunderbolt?'

'Amma, you don't know all that happened there. I shudder to even say it. It is not a matter of a day or two, but five years. His words and his behaviour...enough!' She gestured with finality.

'Whatever it is, he takes care of his wife and child, doesn't he?'

'I can take care of my child and myself. I am a postgraduate.'

'But a child needs the support of a father. Did you think of that? That too...this child.'

'I don't like the name you have given me. I like Meenalochani,' insisted the girl.

'Don't say that, Suthanthira. The name I have given you is such a beautiful one. You will realize that when you grow up.'

The two of them were sitting in the veranda. Suthanthira went to see her on some days even if her grandfather had no work there, because of the friendship that had taken root. She would even put Paappa on her lap and stare at him.

'Why is he like this? He is like a little baby, not speaking, dribbling and staring at the same spot.'

'You know about little babies?'

'Yes, I know. There is a little baby at home, who does not dribble all the time, looks here and there, crawls and calls me "kkaa" already.'

Maybe with his medical treatment, Paappa will also do all that one day. Did the continuation of treatment depend on the financial support afforded by Muthu's job as the manager of a big electronics company?

A cool wind blew from somewhere and played with the leaves of the mango tree in the compound. The mango leaves got drunk with sudden joy and started jumping up and down. Raindrops pierced the sky and fell on the ground releasing a treasure of coolness.

Meenalochani set Paappa on the floor with a thud and ran down with a squeal of joy. She ran towards the tree and started dancing and spinning around. She was wearing a green dress that had been darned. As she spun around, all the green of the earth seemed to smear the green of her dress. Nandu kept looking at her with Paappa tucked between her arms.

Suthanthira danced. Only she could dance…no fetters on her feet…or the dancing Ganesha could. In the tips of her toes that lit up the ground, freedom danced with abandon.

'Appa and Amma want me to get married next month, as soon as I'm through with my BA exams.' After dinner when the English news was over, Kala switched off the TV and sat near her sister. 'They are afraid Ravi and I will cross our limits,' Kala laughed.

'What do his folks say?'

'Ravi's father has agreed. I think his mother is not so happy. She wanted him to marry her brother's daughter. But I feel she will give in to her son's wishes.'

'That's a relief. So the marriage will go off without a hitch, right?'

'That's what, Akka…There should be no hitch, no? I am

afraid his mother will call it off at the slightest excuse.'

'What excuse?'

Kala looked at her and then looked down. 'Don't you know it could be anything? The girl did not do namaskaram properly by touching the elders' feet, the girl's mother was not respectful, or…the girl's sister is a vazhavetti[3] – silly excuses like that…'

Kala tried to smile, but failed. She looked at Nandu once and fell silent.

Nandu stood up.

'I will go check if Paappa has wet himself in his sleep, Kala. I am feeling sleepy too…Good night.'

Nandu took two steps as she headed inside.

'Akka.'

She stopped.

'I love…Ravi…very much.'

One could clearly see the shadow of the dancing statue on the wall behind in the brightness of the night lights. The toe tips danced in delight.

'Amma, will you give me this figurine?'

'But of course. Let the Ganesha bring you good fortune when he enters your house. Let good things happen to you.'

Amma's voice was saturated with love and Nandu melted for a minute. Then despair enveloped her.

Every relationship is beautiful and begins with love…with the husband, with the child, with the sibling. Every bond must be a loving one, enriching one's life. But today, they were all chains that would not allow her to be free to fly towards peace. Her husband, a chain; her child, another chain; and her sibling, yet another.

'Thanks, Amma.'

She placed the Ganesha in her shoulder bag. On the day she set off to return to her husband, she had the child hugging one shoulder, and on the other shoulder was the bag.

Her luggage was loaded on the taxi and Appa hurried her.

'Come on, Nandu. The Brindavan Express will not wait for us. When the taxi came, the clock chimed four – a good omen.'

Appa and Amma behaved as if she were a newly married bride going to her husband. Appa had taken a day off to make sure that her husband would not fly into a rage because she had left him suddenly and come away.

'One minute, Appa. I've asked her to come. There she is.'

Her curly hair flying, her feet so fleet that they did not touch the ground, Suthanthira came running, wearing a brown frock, and stopped, panting hard.

'Suthanthira…'

Nandu knelt down, holding Paappa in her arms. She hugged her and kissed her on her cheek.

'Is this necessary now?' Nandu could hear her Amma mumble, standing on the veranda.

'Shall I go, Suthanthira? Sorry, Meenalochani – you did not like that name, did you?'

'I like it now.' The little girl, who had grown fond of Nandu in these two months, was visibly moved. 'When will you come back?'

'I will come for my sister's wedding.'

'Will he talk then?'

Nandu took out a packet of Cadbury's Gems from her bag.

'Hey! Gems!'

'It is only for you. This is for you too.' She took out the sandstone Ganesha.

'Pillayar Sami.'

'Pillayar Sami who dances.'

'Just for me?'

'Yes. When you grow up and get married, give it to some little girl like you. Shall I go?' She got into the taxi with Paappa.

'Dance, Suthanthira. Like you danced that day in the rain. Dance like that. I'll leave as I watch you dance…'

Suthanthira, tears trembling in her eyes, began to dance… her hands swaying, her body spinning…

ten

Echoes of the Veena

THE OBITUARY IN THE NEWSPAPER hit her hard. She had not known him that well. But a mild shock did course through her, as though a long-forgotten face had suddenly appeared before her with a scar.

Third in the obituary column, she saw the name 'A.P. Jagadeeswara Sarma'.

'The well-known veena vidwan (maestro), Nagapattinam A.P. Jagadeeswara Sarma, who had been unwell for a few months, died last evening at Royapettah Hospital. He was 60 years old. Born in a musical family, he started giving veena concerts from the age of 15. The veena schools established by him in Nagapattinam and Chennai are known for their pure Carnatic tradition-bound training. He composed many devotional songs and created two new ragas (Jagada and Eswari). Though he had performed in numerous concerts and played for many radio programmes, and had a devoted fan following all over India, he never accepted an invitation to go abroad. He won the "Vainikottama" award, the national honour, the Padma Shri, and the Sangeet Natak Akademi award for instrumental music. He is survived by his wife and two sons.'

Her deep sigh fanned her thoughts and her eyelids fluttered. But there was no warmth in that sigh – just tepidness. She did not remember him clearly. In her childhood, she had been through many routines like music and dance tuitions, attending Hindi classes, and he was one of them – the music teacher from whom she learnt the veena for two years. Every Monday and Friday evening, he came home at five-thirty and taught her the veena for two hours. She submitted herself to this routine only because of her parents' keenness to make their daughter an all-rounder in the fine arts. She was not particularly enthusiastic about playing the veena. So she had no regret when the classes were stopped. In fact, she told her parents that she did not want to resume the classes and rid herself of the bother. Yet, just as a child attaches herself to a person who withdraws from her, the treasure of music lovingly buried itself in her reluctant fingers. Jagadeeswaran would drown in wonder as exquisite melodies flowed from her veena. The beauty multiplied many times as an image reflects itself in a four-way mirror.

These memories rose like a dream, with clarity on hearing of his death. Whenever she heard his name on the radio or at a concert, or saw his name in a programme schedule, she would think, 'Oh my old veenai vadhyar!' and forget that equally quickly. Somehow she now felt this gush of compassion on his death. A guru who had ceased to exist thirty years ago had been resurrected. The fact that he had died meant he had lived till then, and had thus come alive. A life full of titles and honours had been lived in a place somewhere. She did not remember reading anywhere that he had received the Sangeet Natak Akademi award! And Padma Shri too? Every year the newspapers would carry the list of the Padma awardees. It was possible to go through the names of the individuals who had been awarded the Padma Vibhushan or Padma Bhushan as there were not many. But the Padma Shri list grew every year and the eyes would scan it superficially. God knows when she missed it. Even the programme notices did not carry the title before his name.

'Are you still reading the newspaper, Rami?'

Ramya lowered the paper, took off her reading glasses and put them on the table when her husband entered the room.

'Nothing. I recognized a name in the obituary column and sat thinking about it.'

'Sad! Who is it?' He gave the standard response to the word 'obituary', and then continued, 'By the way, about the evening light music show – is your friend sure to go with you, as planned? Or should I come?'

'I meant to tell you myself, but it slipped my mind. I invited her because I thought you would get bored at the concert. But it seems she and her family are going to watch *Exorcist* this evening.'

'Once again?'

111

'How does it matter to you? I'm afraid you will have to come with me.'

'Sure. I'll come a little early today. It's at the University Centenary Hall, right?'

'Mmm.'

'When does the programme start?'

'Six.'

'I'll be back.' And he left for office. Ramya smiled to herself.

So many young women even go abroad all by themselves. But she must be accompanied by her husband or a friend to go from Kilpauk to Chepauk! Funny! Poor guy, he always made adjustments for her sake. He hated light music. That did not mean he loved serious Carnatic music. Listening to that had become a habitual ritual…that was all.

The male help had taken leave for two days because of fever. Ramya dusted the sofa and chairs. She carefully arranged the books on the shelf. When the ironing man called at the door, she handed over her washed and starched saris and her husband's clothes. When they were done, she took them in. Then she locked the front door, had her lunch and sat down in her room.

If he listened to Carnatic music as though it were a ritual, she was no better. It was not as if she had any depth of knowledge or keen appreciation of the music. Nothing of the sort. She had a superficial understanding and could recognize a few basic ragas. It was more an aural joy than an intellectual grasp, similar to the way she enjoyed light music. It was not that this was a recent change, even then so many years ago, she had no deep interest in it.

'Wonderful! This is it, this is it! What the fingers play sounds like a human voice. Can such gamaka emerge from an instrument? The veena has come alive,' Jagadeeswaran would rave in wonder, when all she thought was, 'Such a bore, this tuition...and all I want to do is play badminton with Kamala!'

She read the obituary notice again.

Maybe if she had real taste in music and devotion to learn it at that time, she would have understood Jagadeeswaran, the Teacher Sir...maybe? It was only later – many years later – that she realized the truth. Sir had not kissed her fingers, but the goddess of music who dwelt in them.

That day – some thirty years ago – when the evening light and shadows mingled to form a lovely poem, she played 'Mamava Pattabhirama'. The coronation of Rama was brought to life in glorious melody, a manifestation of the sacred spirit of music. And Jagadeeswaran became intoxicated with the beauty, lost himself, and cried: 'Ah...ah! You are Ramya...this is Ramyam...this is enchanting.'

Tears spilled from his eyes as he caught hold of the fingers of her left hand and kissed them passionately. The seventeen-year-old girl was taken aback, was afraid, was immature and incapable of comprehending that this devotee of music was possessed.

'Ayyo Amma!' She yelled.

A terrible scene ensued. Appa slapped him. Amma cursed him.

'We let you in, you teacher chap, only because everyone recommended you as a decent fellow. And you dare do this under the guise of teaching our daughter?' they ranted.

'Step into this house next time and you will see what happens, you rascal!' They chased him out.

'Forgive all of us, sir,' she mentally pleaded with him.

Even at that time she did not hate or abuse the teacher. She was chilled by the fear of coming face-to-face with the unknown. That was a moment when music had transcended the physical limits and become transformed into a primordial truth. She understood that now.

'How hurt must that great artist have felt that day? How pained with humiliation?' The thought rankled with her.

'Forgive all of us, sir.'

'He is survived by his wife and two sons.' Thank god! An unmarried young man's life was not ruined because of her parents. He too had married like everyone else and had children! Thank god!

He died last evening.

Now he would have become ashes.

'This is Ramyam...this is enchanting!!' Those words, the ecstasy on his face that she now remembered with clarity, that pure self which forgot everything in the enchantment that was music...all burnt to ashes.

Poor teacher!

You died, sir?

The huge crowd in the hall was rapt listening to the light

music with the thumping beat. It was K.S. Udayakumar's group with many male and female voices, including a young upcoming female playback singer. Music showered like small flowers gently falling from a tree. The orchestra consisted of the accordion, flute, viola, guitar, drum and mridangam. They sang the lyrics set in light music, new Tamil poets' poems set to music, and Hindi and Tamil film songs.

Ramya was enjoying the music. Next to her sat her husband, yawning behind his hands and frequently checking his watch.

A young man with go-go glasses and flared trousers sang *'Aaj se pehle aaj se jyada'*. After he was done, the leader of the orchestra came forward along with the playback singer.

'Now Ms V. Uma will sing a song of Bharatiyaar's which I have set to raga Eswari. This raga is the creation of Padma Shri awardee, veena vidwan Jagadeeswara Sarma. He passed away last evening. It was purely by chance that I had chosen this raga and it is being performed today as our tribute to his memory,' he announced on the mic.

Bharatiyaar glowed in Eswari.

Oh! Is this Eswari raga? She had heard this before but had not registered the name. A bit like Surati…The crispness of the raga was proof that it was the creation of an instrumentalist who played the swaras alone. Yet it was enchanting.

He had seen before him the enchantment of music as a vision. What intensity even thirty years ago! Truly that life must have been a successful one…a life in which music was truth and truth music. He did not seek publicity for his music by going abroad. He did not prefix his name with the title, Vainikottama, or the honour of Padma Shri. These did not matter to him. He had lived as an artiste to whom music was the worship of Nadam.

'Why shouldn't I offer my condolences to his family?' A teacher she had known long ago, between the time she was fifteen and seventeen. There had been no contact since then. In fact, she had not had any memory of him until now... when it was revived at the news of his death. It would be ridiculous to tell his people that she was deeply saddened. But there was some impulse to express a word of regret and her respect for the great artiste, to indicate that she was aware of his death. Why should she think such impulses were ridiculous? Isn't it possible that such thoughts, which arise in an instant, without any planning, are the purest and most unsullied?

'Many years ago that Jagadeeswara Sarma was my veena teacher for a short while,' she told her husband as they were carried out of the hall by the surge of the crowd.

'Wow! Do you know how to play the veena, Rami? You never told me!'

'I gave it up so long ago and did not remember until now. I must get his address. Will the light music group tell me? How to ask them?'

In the end, she got the address from K.S. Udayakumar himself, having contacted him through someone in charge of the hall. By 4:30 the next day, she reached the house in Vadapalani.

A small house, but it looked attractive, recently whitewashed and with a row of potted croton plants standing in front. Ramya saw that people were moving in and out, maybe to offer their condolences. She waited at the door with hesitation. Two persons came out of the front room. A woman remained there all alone. Not very lean, but of a height that made her seem lean. The white hair was beginning to overtake the black. She was perhaps fifty, but because of her features, her beauty was undimmed. Before one could wonder at how beautiful she looked, her overwhelming grief quelled that awe. She was not wearing any of the inauspicious symbols of a widow. But one could immediately recognize that she was the dead man's wife.

She raised her eyebrows questioningly. Ramya folded her hands in respect.

'I…I am Ramya Mahadevan. My husband works in the Reserve Bank. Many years ago, I was sir's veena student… when I was young. I read the news the day before yesterday, I felt very sad and I wanted to express it in person'

'Oh. Please sit down. I am his wife.'

Sorrow and bitterness overflowed from every word. Sorrow, yes…but why bitterness? It did not look as if she lacked the facilities required to lead a comfortable life. There were chairs, a table, curtains, a reeded mat on the floor, a fan overhead, a radio on the corner stool, a stereo record player nearby and many music records on the open shelf, and the only picture on the wall was of Saraswathi with a veena.

She had come in, leaving her slippers outside, and did not

know what to say after she sat down on the chair. She felt that she should not have come here on an impulse to meet total strangers. Truly why had she come? Let alone coming in person, she did not even know them well enough to compose a condolence note.

He was a teacher who came and 'bored' her twice a week for two years when she was young…a person of no consequence who had crossed her life long ago. That young man of thirty had died long before this man of sixty did. There was no connection between that man and this one as far as she was concerned. Then why had she come? Was it a part of that 'Forgive us, sir'?

'I don't know what to say. I have no words to console you.' She came up with the usual clichés.

'Yes…even I can't believe it. It is overwhelming.' Tears streamed down the woman's eyes. After sobbing for a moment, she collected herself and wiped her tears and fell silent.

Then breaking her silence, she began to speak. 'You know, my first son, Viswam, is not one to get shocked by anything. Whatever the situation may be, he will speak cogently to the people who are with him. He has done his MSc and is working in a company in Kovai. We sent him a telegram when my husband's condition turned critical. He came at once by bus the day before yesterday and the cremation was yesterday. He could stay only for a day. He left last night, saying he will apply for leave and come for the rituals on the tenth day and thereafter. His company will not give him leave at all – they depend on him. He is only twenty-six, but has already earned a place for himself. The head office at Chennai has selected him for an assignment abroad. He is so brilliant. He has even accepted it.'

Ramya was taken aback by this outpouring.

'I read that sir was ailing for some months,' Ramya began, but the other interrupted her.

'Wasn't it mentioned that he was a Padma Shri awardee? I was the one who said that they simply must mention it. Many people don't even know that. Do you?'

'I got to know only from the paper.'

'See…'

'What was he suffering from?'

'Diabetes, and hypertension too. When did he ever take care of himself? He was running between Chennai and Nagapattinam for the sake of these wretched veena schools. He would forget his diet and medicine. When he was here, I would take care of him. I told him not to strain like that. I told him the schools are fairly well established and others will take care of them. I told him he should relax. But he did not listen. His world was only music; that was his only passion.' She sighed and stopped.

'He is survived by his wife and two sons.'

'What happened in the end?' asked Ramya softly.

'Diabetic carbuncle…could not be operated. The medicines did not work and gangrene set in. He had a fever. We rushed to the Royapettah hospital. He slipped into a coma two days after that. That was all.'

She wiped her eyes again.

'I sent Viswam a telegram as soon he went into a coma. He set off at once. It seems he did not get a bus ticket on an emergency basis. But he managed, he said. He is that capable...very intelligent. Does the company send everyone on assignments abroad? It may even be America, I believe. A matter of pride, no?'

Ramya stared at her

'Amma,' a young man came calling, and stopped on seeing Ramya.

'This is the younger one, Balu, BA, looking for a job. I tell him what is the hurry to get a job – he should try for a scholarship to study abroad,' said Jagadeeswaran's wife.

'Are your two sons interested in Sir's veena schools?'

'Where do they have the time for that? Viswam is focused only on his work. Otherwise, would he have made such a name for himself as to get the chance to go abroad? This fellow is worried about getting a job. Hey, Balu! Where are you coming from? You went in the morning after immersing the ashes and then taking a bath, and you've returned only now. Where have you been roaming? Wouldn't it be helpful to me if you stayed at home to meet those who come to offer their condolences? The two of you are my only support now. Your father has left me to fend for myself.' Tears again. Balu gritted his teeth and went away.

A taxi stopped outside, Ramya noted...more mourners. She stood up.

'You must be brave and take heart, at least for your sons.' Ramya hated herself for mouthing these clichés.

'Oh! Leaving? Can you do me a favour?' The veena exponent's wife wiped her eyes and stood up.

'What?'

'There is this big veena that he played. It is a decorated, antique one. I think it will fetch a high price. Can you ask any of the big people you know if they would buy it? Please come in, see it and tell me how much it would be worth. Since you were his student, you may know about veenas. Your husband may also have rich acquaintances since he works in the Reserve Bank.'

Ramya was speechless. She kept looking at the woman before her. She steadied herself with some effort.

'Sorry. It has been a long time since I have lost touch with the veena. Now I don't know anything about veenas.'

She got into the taxi from which the passengers had got off and gave the driver her address. The vehicle started. She leaned back and stared blankly.

Sir, you have really died.

'It seems the man who died was a great veena player…a pity.' The taxi driver was a chatty young man. He darted like an arrow between two buses.

'Yes.'

'Two children, they said.' he continued.

'Yes. Jagada and Eswari.'

eleven

I am Meenatchi

Y OUR NAME? – *Maitreyi.*
   Yours? – Lakshmibai, Rani of Jhansi.
Yours? – Padmini, Rani of Chittor.
What's your name? – Florence Nightingale.
And yours? – Joan of Arc.
Yours? – Helen Keller, Ida Scudder, Emmeline Pankhurst, Jane Austen, Amrita Sher-Gil, Annie Besant, Sister Subbulakshmi, Panditha Ramabai, Lata Mangeshkar.

And many, many more. All women of renown. From Vedic times to today's cricket player, Shanta Rangaswami ... all the names are mine. That is why when I was in school, immersed in my dreams, I would not answer to my name, S. Meenatchi, during roll call, and had my head chewed off by my teachers.

Who was this S. Meenatchi? She had my face and my form, but I was not merely her. I was going to fly with my wings of fame. That had been my dream since childhood, so that was the

inner me. Was this S. Meenatchi one of the numerous Meenatchis?
Not at all. I was Sarasavani...Saradhamani...Soodikoduththa
Sudarkodi-Aandal.

'Meena!'

Amma's frail voice disturbed her train of thought. She stopped rocking on the swing and went in.

Amma was stirring something on the gas stove.

'Did Appa tell you...the good news?'Amma asked with a smile.

'What about?'

'Silly girl! It is about your marriage, of course. Those people who saw you last week have said they liked you. I am not at all surprised. That boy could not take his eyes off you. You just entranced him.'

Pride and joy bubbling inside her, Amma stroked Meenatchi's left cheek, without halting her work. Meena felt an instant thrill. The refined face of that man came before her eyes. She would enslave him, like Cleopatra, like Nur Jahan.

'Didn't Appa tell you?'

'No, Amma.'

'What haven't I told her?' asked Appa, as he entered the room.

'That the Bangalore people have written that they liked her.'

'Oh! You have already given her the news? I was just coming in to tell her. Don't you know that I am the one who should announce all important information?'

The joy drained out of Amma's face.

123

'Don't get angry. I thought that you would have told her since it is something to be happy about, and that is why I asked her.'

'Impertinent and hasty. Are you chopping beans? Today I feel like having pudalangai koottu. So make just that.'

After Appa had gone, Meena looked at Amma with pity. Without a word, Amma put the chopped beans away and started cutting the snake gourd. Meena had never seen Amma ignoring Appa's orders. Doing his bidding all these years had worn her out. After bearing five children, her body looked emaciated. Her forehead, her eyes and the natural grace of her thin frame indicated that she must have been beautiful once. Everyone who praised Meena's good looks also noted that she resembled her mother.

Where did Amma's beauty disappear? Had it got lost in the labour of five births, in the drudgery of performing the daily chores, and in the fear of facing Appa, which made her shrink? The ash from the joss stick takes the same form when it falls. But that form is not the fragrant stick; it is just the burnt-out ash.

In the next few days the house buzzed with talk of the marriage. Meena was in a dream of ecstasy. She was quite surprised to note that she, a postgraduate, a bank officer, and a person who borrowed loads of books from the library and read deeply, was as smitten as any ordinary girl by the thought of getting married. She reasoned with herself that it was not wrong to be happy, and not wrong to get married. Joan of Arc may have been unmarried, but the queen of

Jhansi was married, wasn't she? Can marriage shroud one's excellence and one's qualifications? Can you cover the glow of the beautiful lamp?

I am Madame Curie. I have won the Nobel Prize with my husband and shown to the world that married life could be like this too.

'Appada!' She heaved a sigh of relief as she put the books down on the swing. Two of them were biographies —one about Madame Montessori and the other about Mother Teresa. If only she could be like them…creating a new system of education for young minds or wiping the tears of orphans in the name of god.

'Here Meena, drink your coffee and then read.'

'Oh! I'm sorry, Amma. I should have come in and taken it instead of troubling you.' Meena took the coffee from her mother.

'The book has kept you hooked, that's why.'

'Yes.'

'I know. When I was your age, I too was like that, especially if they were Sanskrit books.'

'Sanskrit books? You used to read Sanskrit? I can't believe it.'

'Your Thaatha – that is, my Appa – was a great pandit of Sanskrit, right? He taught that divine language to all of us so well. He was very proud that I was his best student. He gave all his books – the epics, the plays and the poems – only to me. I would read them again and again, oblivious of the passage of time.'

She had never seen her mother read a Sanskrit book in her life. In fact, she had never seen one at home.

She was just going to ask her about it, when her Appa came along.

'Hey, Meena. There is another letter from the Bangalore people.'

Though she was curious, she just lifted her head silently.

'The boy likes you. But he does not like you working. He wants you to give up your job.'

'What is this, Appa? I will not do it.' Meena was shocked.

'Don't talk rubbish. You started working just for the fun of it. Do you have to work for a living? You must not reject a good alliance for this reason. He is handsome and well-placed. They are decent people. They are not asking for any dowry. It is our good fortune that this alliance came our way.'

Meena seethed and simmered for a long time. Finally, the knot inside her resolved itself. It was not as if she absolutely loved the bank job. After she had got her MA degree, she had seen the advertisement and taken the bank exam. She had passed the written examinations easily and the viva too, and then the job was hers. But what great soul satisfaction would she derive from a desk job? This was not something to which she could dedicate herself. (*I am Mary Verghese, I am Muthulakshmi Reddy.*) It would be no big loss to give up the job. In these days of increasing unemployment, her working for the heck of it was actually akin to stealing from some man or woman who was the head of a family and really needed that income.

She agreed to give up the job. And the marriage preparations gathered momentum.

'Is this mango raw or ripe?' Appa yelled.

'Why? Is it sour? I heard the man selling mangoes outside. I bought it because you like them. It is so yellow, and smells good. Isn't it sweet?'

'It is like you. You can use it if there is no tamarind at home. And she says she bought mangoes for me. If you don't know a thing, why don't you just keep quiet? Why burn hard-earned money? Now did I ask you to buy mangoes for me? Hmm? Throw them into the garbage.'

Why is Appa like this? Amma would have been overjoyed if he had only said, 'It is a bit sour. But you thought of me and that is what matters.'

She was reading late into the night, when Amma came in.

'Meena, still awake? It is going to be two.'

'Why are you awake till two?'

'I don't know, I'm just unable to sleep. Don't stay up for long. You have to go to work tomorrow. Moreover, if the bride-to-be does not sleep well, her eyes will look sunken. And that will ruin your looks. This is the time when you must eat well, sleep well and be happy.'

'Yes, Amma. But I forget the world when I start reading.'

'I know. I understand.'

Meena suddenly remembered the conversation that was interrupted that day.

'Amma, why don't you read Sanskrit now? No time? I want to hear you read Sanskrit. All these days I did not know you were such a learned pandit. Where are the books Thaatha gave you?'

'They are with the used books seller'

'Why?'

'Appa's orders. He didn't like me reading Sanskrit, a language he did not know. He said, "You want to show off your knowledge, is it? Not anymore. Just tie them up in a bundle and dump them in the old book shop." This happened 25 years ago. It is the silver jubilee of the demise of my Sanskrit.'

Amma's face was void of any expression. Meena hugged her.

'What is this…like a little child? Close the book, switch off the lamp and go to sleep.'

Amma stroked her hair lovingly and withdrew from her arms.

That night Meena again became a schoolgirl in her dream.

'S. Meenatchi… S. Meenatchi… Why no response? Absent?'

'No, Miss. I am here. But my name is not Meenatchi. I am Maria Montessori, I am Mother Teresa. I am Bala Saraswathi, Shakuntala Devi…Sarojini Naidu.'

The month of the marriage was approaching when another letter arrived from Bangalore.

'Meena, there is a letter from the bridegroom. He likes you, he writes, but it seems his mother is orthodox. So she wants you to pierce your nose. "Please do this for my mother. It will make me happy," he says. We will call a goldsmith to pierce your nose tomorrow. Then I will write to Bangalore.'

Appa then turned to Amma.

'Get everything ready for the nose-piercing ceremony.'

'What nonsense! No nose-piercing, tongue-piercing. I don't like it – I won't do it.' Meena was full of indignation.

'What is wrong with piercing your nose? You will look like Goddess Lakshmi. They will present you with a diamond nose ring.'

'I won't do it, Appa. They knew when they saw me that my nose was not pierced. Why didn't they say no? Why didn't they say they do not want a girl without a pierced nose?'

'If your nose were crooked, they would have said no. But this is something that can be changed – why should they reject you for that? It is only because they like you that they have gone this far. Do not make a song and a dance about such a trivial thing. I will call the goldsmith tomorrow. Be ready.'

It took a long while for Meena's temper and protest to subside. When Amma asked her not to make a fuss and to let go, she calmed down. When she thought about it, she felt that it was indeed a trivial matter. Now nose rings are becoming quite the fashion too. It is not a big deal to say yes. Her heart leapt with joy when she imagined how that young man's face would look much more radiant and handsome on seeing her nose adorned with a ring. When she looked at herself in the mirror, humming softly, she felt very happy.

What will I look like with a nose ring?

She sprinkled some face powder on her palm. With that, she made a white dot on her nose. It looked as if she were wearing a huge pearl nose ring. She looked lovely. She had never imagined it would suit her so well. Wow! He would faint with happiness when he saw her…it was for his sake.

She stood looking at her reflection in the mirror for some time. Who was this woman? This face and the nose ring…It was Amma…just like her. Just like her only to look at…Or?

Amma who had never defied Appa, Amma who had wilted without any love from Appa, Amma who had celebrated the silver jubilee of the destruction of her aspirations and desires.

'Throw the Sanskrit books away.'

'Yes, I will.'

Then I…I…how am I different?

Want me to resign from my job? – Yes, I will.

Want me to pierce my nose? – Yes, I will.

She teetered on the edge of all that she had dreamt of from her childhood. From there, she saw the reality of the chasm below. The reality hit her and her whole self was aflame with fear.

She would never become the Rani of Jhansi or Mother Teresa. She would not become any of those countless women. If she continued like this, she would only become another Amma. The moulding of Meenatchi into her mother's image had already begun.

But the form had not hardened yet.

She sat up and wrote a letter to Bangalore.

'I will not pierce my nose. I will not leave my job. If you want to marry me as I am, that is fine. If not, I am afraid I have to say no to you.'

She sealed the cover and placed it on the table. She would post it first thing in the morning.

Calm sleep enveloped her as she realized with a thrill that she had stepped back from the cliff's edge.

Who are you? – Me. It's me.

What's your name? – S. Meenatchi.

S. Meenatchi! – Present.

twelve

The Lonely Fledgling

A LITTLE GIRL ALL ALONE in this entire universe; a little girl standing forever in the large garden of her Paatti's house amidst the mango, guava and magizham trees stirring the loneliness on this earth and in the sky above.

'Hey, Kannagi! How long has it been since you came back from school? Come in, change out of your school clothes, drink your milk and then go. Go wherever you want to.' Paatti's voice commanded, but Kannagi knew that it was drenched in affection. That did not take away her loneliness.

She took off her school uniform, wore her usual clothes, and had her milk and snacks. After that, she sat near the curve of the staircase and did her homework; after that, she heard her Paatti's stories; after that, she had her dinner; after that, she went to sleep; after that, she woke up; after that, she went to school; after that, she returned…It was loneliness alone that remained in the end.

132

The soothing chirping of birds at dawn; the cuckoo cooing sweetly from the mango tree; the diamond spark-like raindrops that spattered on the ground from the mango leaves after a dense rain that bridged the sky and earth, leaving no gap; the streaking colours of sunset setting the evening sky on fire again. It was less warm now. Joy spurted at the bottom of her heart at what she saw. She turned to share it with someone, but with who...Thaatha...Paatti...servants...classmates? No...no. None of them held any meaning for her; they were not the company she wanted. In an instant, the loneliness she had forgotten would loom again like a demon and spread itself inside all the beautiful sights she had seen.

When she heard the call of the postman, she would be the first at the door. Her eyes would scan the addresses on the envelopes in the postman's outstretched hand.

'What child, want to know if there is a letter for you? Expecting a love letter at this age?' the postman teased her with the liberty that his age gave him. Kannagi would not move. Her eyes remained fixed on the envelopes. Some days, her face drooped at once. But on a few other days, she thrilled at the sight of the awaited handwriting. She would hover around her grandparents.

'What is it, girl? What keeps you here? Isn't it time for school?'

'Just leaving.'

It was what she pined for, longed for and prayed for.

'Here, a letter for you, too.' She pined, longed for and prayed that one day Thaatha would say there was a letter for her too, a tiny paper stuck inside their letter, like a little kangaroo tucked in her mother's pouch.

'You got up so early. What do you mean by lazing around since then? If you get ready quickly, you can go to school early, right? Your Paatti finished cooking so long ago. And you come to her to have your hair plaited at eight?' Thaatha scolded her.

She silently got ready to go to school.

'Kannagi!'

'What Paatti?' She came with a gush of eagerness, her heart beating fast, waiting to hold out her hand, but she restrained herself.

She must hold her hand out only after Paatti said there was a letter for her.

'This morning, you forgot to drink your Bournvita after brushing your teeth. Such forgetfulness! They used to ask in jest if we will forget to eat. But you actually do it. After having your food, you must drink that before going.'

On her way to school, with a broken heart and her bag in hand, loneliness trailed her like a shadow.

Some days, she heard Paatti and Thaatha talking to each other.

'Veni has written a letter.'

'What does she say?'

'It seems our son-in-law was not well.'

'Ay-yay-yo!'

'Don't get alarmed…he is better now.'

'What was wrong with him?'

'He had a constant cough for two months and they were worried it might be TB or something. But fortunately, it was nothing like that…Just an ordinary cough.'

'I suppose he is fully okay now.'

'Yes, he is.'

'What else has she written?'

'Nothing. The usual stuff in one line – if we are all fine. What is there to keep writing about again and again? She too writes only if there is some news like this.'

'That's fine. Has she written at least a line about Kannagi?'

'What's there to write about her? She knows the child is in good care with us.'

'Even then…I just asked if there was a line about Kannagi.'

'The enquiry about us includes the child, does it not?'

That day, the demon of loneliness sprouted ten heads.

On rare occasions, she heard the words, 'She has enquired about Kannagi,' or 'She has asked if Kannagi has done well in her exams.' Paatti would then call her and tell her that her mother had enquired about her. And when she did that, Paatti's voice and eyes acquired a special softness. Kannagi felt as if that deep look had entered her heart and melted as tears. Kannagi would stiffly say 'Mmm' and run to the magizha tree and sit under its shade, drowning in the sweetness of those words. Paatti would not call her in for a long time.

'You say you are with your Thaatha and Paatti. Don't you have Appa and Amma?'

'I do.'

'Oh!'

'Where?'

'In Nagpur.'

'It is a big city. There should be good schools there.'

'Mmm.'

'Then? Do your parents have many children?'

'No, only me.'

'Then is your mother an invalid?'

'Not at all. She is fine, plump, fair and beautiful.'

'What does your father do?'

'He is a big IAS officer.'

'Then they must be well-off. Have you been to Nagpur?'

'I go during my holidays.'

'Do your parents come to Madras often?'

'Nnno…once in a way.'

'How long have you been with your grandparents?'

'Always.'

'After they left you here, how many times have they come?'

'Once.'

The interrogator's eyebrows rose. This must have led Kannagi to sense something; she said hurriedly, 'My parents are very good.'

On the days she visited a friend and had such encounters with the friend's mother, the smouldering embers would be fanned.

Appa, Amma! Appa, Amma!

Amma! Amma! Amma!

Her heart would jump with joy when going to Nagpur. But there…

'Come, Kannagi…How are you? Oh, oh! Your hair looks so dirty and unkempt. As soon as we go home, bathe well with soap. You do bathe, don't you? Or will you always be dirty?'This was Appa, with a laugh.

'You look thin. Do you eat well? If you say no, Paatti will let you off indulgently. That won't work with me. I hope you have brought your schoolbooks. There is no need to be idle during your holidays. You must study daily.' Amma's orders.

She desperately felt like hugging them tight. What if she did just that? Even if they did not like it, once she had hugged them, they could not take that away, right? She felt as if her head would burst if she did not bury herself in her mother.

Once, just once she did it.

'Che, che! How can you fall all over me with the train grime? My sari will get crushed. Did you learn this nonsense in your Madras school?'

After that, she had never hugged her mother at the railway station. But one night, unable to bear the deep need, she hugged her mother and cried on her lap.

Her mother sat her up.

'Kannagi, aren't you ashamed of yourself? Why are you crying? You know I don't like it if you cry like this. Silly… aren't you a big girl now? What is this?'

Her parents would take her out in the car. Amma sat in the front, while Appa drove. She sat alone in the back on the edge of the seat, not leaning back. With her hands gripping the front seat, she imagined that she was sitting in front with them.

137

Once when she was sitting like that, her father braked suddenly. She dashed against the front seat and fell down. She had hurt her chin and it throbbed with pain. Appa glared at her angrily.

'It's my chin…it hurts.' Afraid of him, she mumbled, hoping to subdue his anger.

'Idiot! Why the hell can't you sit upright? If you don't, you will fall and hurt yourself. Do I have to keep checking on you before applying the brakes? Do you want me to hit the vehicle that is coming towards me? I will never take you out if you can't sit properly.'

Kannagi's lips throbbed. She looked at her mother, but Amma remained quiet and did not speak on her behalf. Kannagi leaned back. When the car started again, she burst into tears. No one stopped her from crying. They must have thought that she was crying because her chin hurt.

She roamed around the house all through the holidays, like a satellite revolving separately and a little away from the world of her parents. They would bestow a smile on her as though they suddenly remembered her existence in their life of togetherness.

'Eat well, Kannagi. This cheese is delicious. Your mother just loves it and can gobble a whole packet, no Veni?' Appa would wink playfully at Amma.

'Tonight we are going to a movie, Kannagi. You can't come because it is the second show. Don't be afraid. Just go to sleep like a good child.' Kannagi kept her head bent as Appa spoke.

'Amma, you always write to Thaatha and Paatti. Once in a

while, write to me too, please,' she said shyly and hesitantly to her mother once when returning after her holidays.

'What can I write to you, my dear? If there is something, I tell them and they will tell you. I keep asking them about you frequently. What can I write to you separately? You are still a child.'

Kannagi looked at her mother, eyes wide and chin wobbling but she did not cry and she never broached this subject again.

They would send her back with friends who were going to Madras.

'Take care, Kannagi. As soon as you reach Madras, ask Thaatha or Paatti to write to us, okay? Ta-ta!' They rushed to a movie or some restaurant even before the train left.

And still she never stopped yearning and the postman's visits to her Thaatha's house were always another sunrise every time.

'No love letter for you, my child!'

She would rush to the guava, mango and magizham trees to battle with her loneliness.

When the next holidays would be round the corner, life would peep out of Kannagi's eyes again.

'Paatti, will the magizham flowers remain fresh for two days?'

'They won't fade. That is, the fragrance will not go.'

'Then can I take a strand of magizham flowers when I go this time?'

'That is a good idea.' Paatti gave an easy smile.

Kannagi looked at the flowers that had fallen in a circle around the tree, gathered them, inhaled their fragrance and pressed their softness against her cheeks.

It was the day of her departure. The train would leave at night. She took out her needle and thread and strung the flowers. Her joy knew no bounds when she had strung a big strand. She was thrilled that she was going to take such a precious gift.

'Kannagi! A letter from your mother has come just now.'

She rushed eagerly on hearing the voice, but when she saw her Paatti's face, her eagerness subsided and an unknown anxiety gripped her.

'It seems the children in the neighbourhood there have chickenpox and your mother, too, is just recovering from it. So she wants to cancel your trip because she does not want you to come now.'

Kannagi stood staring and Paatti's sorrow grew. She pulled Kannagi close to her and spoke to her gently.

'Don't be upset, darling. Mahamayi – the goddess of small pox – is contagious. It is only out of concern for you that your mother has asked you not to come. Don't worry. This time, you, me and Thaatha will go somewhere else, okay? You have never been to Madurai, Thiruvananthapuram or Kanyakumari. We will go somewhere like that and you will love it. Just see.'

Kannagi wilted a bit, but soon recovered and went to the garden. Four or five mangoes had been pecked by the birds and fallen on the ground. She sat under the magizham tree and remained motionless for a long time.

Her friend was surprised when she visited her in the afternoon. Kannagi was not one to go visiting casually.

'Kannagi! Have you come to say goodbye?'

'No. Here, take this.'

She gave her the magizham strand, folded in her kerchief.

'Why are you giving me this?'

'Give it to your Amma.'

'Why all of a sudden? Don't you want to wear it?'

'I strung it only for Amma, so take it.'

She gave her the strand and did not remain there a second longer. She did not sleep that night. In fact, it was many nights before she could sleep.

This was vacation time and it was unusual for her to spend it in Madras. There was nothing to do. Roaming around in the garden and staring at the vacant space became the routine occupations. Paatti told her new stories and played a dice game, a board game and the game of 'goat and tiger' with her. She sent Kannagi to a veena school as a temporary student. She asked Thaatha to plan for a short trip around south India for the three of them. Thaatha taught her the songs by the Tamizh saints Thevaara paasuram, Tiruppavai and Tiruvembavai.

She took part in everything, but loneliness enveloped her at all times.

Days passed and the months too as she wandered aimlessly under the huge trees in the garden, all by herself, a solitary child in this entire universe.

'Veni has written a letter.'

'What does she say?'

'Her husband has been promoted and they are going to Delhi.'

'Promotion? I'm happy. When are they going?'

'End of this month. But it will take a while for them to get their quarters.'

'Then Veni will be here till then, won't she?'

'No. They are going together and she will be with him in the guest house till the quarters are allotted.'

'Why can't she come and stay here? During these holidays, the child has not even gone there. If she came here now, she could at least spend some time with the child, isn't it?'

'You know her. Will she leave him and come, and will your son-in-law let her go?'

'Yes...this pair is a special pair! Never seen the likes of them!'

The darkness that engulfed Kannagi that night was more severe than ever. Even the stars that could usually be seen through the window had been snuffed out. Darkness rose in waves from the cloud clusters that covered the sky. Soon the darkness spread fully across the sky and having filled it, overflowed onto the trees and slithered down the leafy slopes to the ground. Battered here and there by the wind, it dashed against the walls and climbed into her room through the window and covered her completely. Gnawed somewhere by the impact of her sobs, her body was bruised. The tears rose silently like a thin line, gradually gathered strength and loudness as they climbed to the top of her head and burst in a rising crescendo, flooding not just her pillows but the night itself.

'Amma…Amma…Amma.'

In that bottomless blackness, Paatti's arms hugged her gently, soothing like a sprinkle of cool rose water.

'Don't cry, my dear child! Amma will come. Just see…she will come one day. Don't cry…aren't you my pet?…Don't cry.'

School…food…sleep…Paatti's stories…Thaatha's songs paasuram…the garden trees.

Time ticked on…

Now Kannagi had grown tall. There were new depths in her eyes that spoke of her loneliness. Her self-absorption as she sat under the magizha tree had new meanings. There were signs of a cool light, as though the moon had risen in her heart.

'See you, Paatti!' As she shouted with her school bag slung on her shoulders, the postman came.

'Give this to your grandmother, my child. Oh! Not a child any more. You may really get a love letter now.'

Paatti opened the letter as the postman went away. Kannagi had reached the front gate, when an excited voice stopped her.

'Kannagi! Come back! There is good news!'

She went back.

'My child, no more yearning for your parents. Didn't I tell you that your mother would come and you should not worry? She is coming next week and will be here for ten days. Not just that. It seems hereafter you can be with them.

143

Kannagipponnu need never be separated from her parents. She will be with them always.'

Kannagi is grown up. Your son-in-law has no objection to her staying with us now.

Scenes from the past unfolded before the old woman's eyes when she read these lines. Veni, the baby and the cradling function. The son-in-law comes on a visit. Veni complains to her mother, 'Amma, he says that this child is a nuisance. This child will intrude into our life, be a hurdle to our happiness.' Veni weeps. Yet a month later, Veni implicitly obeys her husband when he asks her to return at once, leaving the child with her parents. Has the imprint of her love faded with time, or is it like live embers covered with ash? Or has she too, by association, become like her husband, who cannot rise above his physical needs? When she says that this grown up child can stay with them because she will no longer be a nuisance, what does Veni really feel?

'Kannagi, darling why are you quiet? Did you hear what I said? Your mother! She is going to take you to Delhi! You can be with them to your heart's content!'

Kannagi stood looking at her Paatti. Her face was dotted with perspiration. She let her school bag slip down. She came forward and hugged her Paatti tightly round the waist.

'Paatti, I don't want to go away. I want to be only with you…!'

thirteen

The Mother Smiled

THE JOSS STICK WITH ITS TINY orange flame glowed like a solitary kanakambara flower. Gayathri inhaled the fragrance deeply with a put-on sadness.

'The stick will fade away slowly after exhaling its fragrance in smoke, and so too my life,' she said with a smile.

She was bedridden, her strength diminished by illness. Even then the artificiality of her speech had not diminished. That was a facet of her personality.

'Amma, you are going to live for many more years. Why are you getting so agitated? Just sleep for a while. Poor thing, you rarely sleep after midnight,' said Mani.

'Why do you say sleep for a while? I'm going to sleep for a long time…in fact, forever.'

Mani did not say anything.

'Do you think I'm young? By this October I will be sixty… waiting to welcome death with open arms.'

Mani looked at his mother thoughtfully.

Had his mother fashioned her whole life as a stage on which she mouthed dialogues for the benefit of others? Even her appearance seemed to be made up. No one would believe that she was sixty. No wrinkles on her face, her body was firm and her skin was radiant. If she bit a stone, it would be the stone that would break and not her strong teeth. Even after she turned forty, her eyesight had not deteriorated and she did not have to wear glasses. It was just in the last four or five years that a few grey hair had appeared among the black ones, as though her age had suddenly remembered itself.

She was young when fate dealt her an unjust blow, and it seemed as if that young person decided to remain a stubborn witness, visible to all, to that injustice. Why else would a person crushed by tragedy forever wear that youthful look?

'Even Yama, the god of death, won't know you are sixty, so he will go past you.'

Gayathri stared at her son for a while.

The face on the pillow was without a ripple, like water in a tank. How fair and beautiful she looked! Even the bare forehead, without kumkum, shone with an inherent purity and looked as if the sculptor had felt that any extra detail would detract from the simplicity of the perfection.

Gayathri stretched out her hand to her son, who was sitting close to her.

'But you have become old, my dear one.'

'Amma, I'm only forty-two.'

'But I haven't got you married, cursed that I am!' She

heaved a sigh.

'I am fo…rty-two, Amma,' Mani laughed.

'I don't know about that, you are still my child. If you were married, with a wife and child, if I had seen you as a garlanded groom, would I not have jumped with joy, completely cured, as though I had drunk nectar?'

Gayathri did not realize that she was lying.

'Was that her greatest tragedy?' This was the question that Mani often asked himself.

'Don't think like that, Amma. I am extremely happy just being your son.'

The flash in her unwrinkled young eyes was a flash of triumph!

'Are you speaking the truth, dear? Do you never ever regret that you haven't got married or that you do not have a life of your own?'

'No.' A calm reply.

Wasn't she satisfied? Why did her face not shine fully?

'When I have a mother like you, how can I miss anyone else? It is enough that I have you.'

How many times must he have repeated this to her!

He was rewarded for his words by the intense joy that spread over her face. What else did he need? And, indeed, what else did she have?

But forcing her radiant face to droop at once, she picked up his hand and stroked it.

'Hmm, you are a good child. That's why you say that. But as long as I fail in my duty as a parent, am I not culpable?

Tomorrow, if god asks me why my son did not have a spouse beside him when he performed the last rites for me…what answer will I have?'

Did this anxiety too lurk in the corner of her heart?

'God won't ask such questions. Won't He know?'

'Even now…even now…if you wish it, why don't you get married?'

Mani's fingers touched his grey hair, spectacles and his sunken eyes, and he laughed.

'Amma, if you are old, I am three-fourths there. A marriage for me…now? I do not have any such desire.'

'Sure?'

'Sure.'

'You have never had such a desire?'

'I am yours and yours alone. I do not have any desire beyond being your son.'

Again the triumphant gleam on the beautiful face.

'Whatever you say. If that is your wish, what can I say?' Gayatri smiled at him again.

This exchange was a daily ritual. Neither did she tire of asking her son these things, nor did he tire of responding to his mother.

Ranganathan, the cook, came in with a glass of milk.

'Have you finished all your work?' Gayathri asked him.

'Over, Amma.'

'I'll get the milk for you.' Mani got up.

She reluctantly released her grip over his hand.

Mani took the glass from Ranganathan with his left hand.

148

This was not out of disrespect, but his nature. He was left-handed, that was all. He raised his mother's head with his right hand and with his left, put the glass to her lips. This was something he did for his mother every day. Gayathri sipped it slowly, looking at him all the while.

'They say it is lucky to be left-handed. But you are an exception. That's why you were born to me.'

'I haven't lost anything by being your son.'

He placed the empty glass on the table, wiped her lips with the cloth in his left hand and gently laid her back on the bed.

'Shall I take leave then?' It was the cook.

'Mmm.'

Ranganathan came to work at six in the morning and returned at night after finishing his work. This had been his routine for the last fifteen years. His house was close by, just two streets away. But due to age, he could not see properly in the dark any more, so Mani had been escorting him home for five years now.

'Shall I go with him, Amma?' Mani got up.

'Okay, dear. But come soon. I feel so lost without you.'

He was his mother's focus, life and achievement.

Gayathri was not even eighteen when her husband had died. Two months later, she had turned eighteen and her son was born.

Some pitied him for being a posthumous baby, some cursed him for 'finishing off' his father even before his birth. Amidst all the people who made various comments in those

149

days, Gayathri sat like a stone for hours, staring at him.

'What would that eighteen-year-old girl have thought?' Mani often wondered.

Would she have thought, 'Why this additional burden when life has come to an end?' or, 'This is the sole comfort, being proof of the fact that even in a short life, I lived fully'?

When one is at an age at which one is throbbing with the desire to live, when even the limits of one's dreams are unclear, and a menacing fate puts an end to life even before it has begun, is it possible to deceive oneself into thinking that this is the symbol or the proof of the fullness of one's life? His mother was after all a person made of flesh and blood.

It would not have been surprising if she had hated his father for cruelly dying so suddenly. The sweetness that she had tasted had now been taken away from her forever, and the deprivation was that much more unbearable. The child was a gentle reminder of that sweetness and the loss, and so it would not be surprising if she had hated the child too.

When that young woman, who was forcibly imprisoned in an unnatural barrenness, had sat staring at her child, slowly, unbeknownst to her, a bond of hatred might have been forged in her heart. That too would not be surprising. Her love must have been three-fourths hatred.

When she had lost everything, the only thing that justified her existence was her child. If she lost him too, the only testimony to her horrendous fate would have gone. It was only by binding him to herself that she could spit triumphantly into the face of Fate, which had been cruel to her.

Mani also understood that she would not be aware of the logic of all that she thought. She was certainly not conscious that her every thought and deed arose involuntarily from her, a prisoner of her tragedy and devastation. She must have thought she was an independent being. She must have thought she had nothing but love for the child whom she had carried and hugged in her arms.

His grandfather – father's father – had taken care of them. He had made a will with the intention of securing his daughter-in-law's future after his death.

Mani turned twenty-four. Thaatha found a good bride for his grandson.

When he told Gayathri that the alliance was a good one and that the family would be supportive of her, she accepted it respectfully, with her head bent. She appeared to be happy with the arrangement. But her eyes were restless. When Mani looked at her by chance, he saw a crazed confusion in her expression. She was always talking to herself, as though in a delirium, hiding her thoughts in her words.

'Just two weeks more. My daughter-in law will be here. I will then be free of care. I will derive total bliss from watching the pair.'

'Just ten days more. My daughter-in-law will be here.'

'Just eight days more. My daughter-in-law will be here.'

Whenever he woke up in the night, he saw his mother wide awake on her bed, or staring at the sky in the terrace, or walking ceaselessly in the room.

'Amma, not able to sleep?'

'No. I'm just overflowing with joy. Just five days more. My daughter-in-law will be here. You will be her husband.' Then she would stare at his face and without a warning, a question would be unsheathed like a penknife.

'But you will still be my son, right?'

'Why do you doubt that, Amma?'

Did he comprehend her then? Otherwise, why was he now flooded with a gush of pity and sorrow for her? Otherwise, why did he feel a kind of relief along with the sense of loss when his Thaatha died of a heart attack three days before the wedding, and his mother called off the wedding, citing that as a reason and saying that the girl had brought misfortune?

For the next two years no one raised the topic of his marriage. Then there were murmurs and comments from the neighbours.

'Why are you postponing what you should do for your son?'

'He is earning well and he is young. If you don't get him married, he will go astray.'

'Just because you look so young, does it mean you should not get a daughter-in-law?'

Unable to bear this, one day she said, 'I have no objection. Please suggest a good girl.'

A suitable girl was found when he was twenty-seven. Gayathri had rejected many girls for one reason or the other. Finally, there came a proposal which even she could not object to and she fell silent.

Again the restlessness and the palpitations and the

sleepless nights…and the exaggerated liveliness and also, the counting of days in a state of agitation.

'Just twenty-six days more, just twenty-five days more.'

The girl died in an accident twelve days before the wedding, as if nothing else could have stopped the marriage.

'Every time your wedding is fixed, something like this happens. Why?' What was there on her wrinkle-free, young face – surprise, sorrow, a stirring or relief? Was it just a feeling of comfort that she didn't have to lose her son? Or was it also a release from anxiety for a person who had been condemned to loneliness from youth, who could not bear to see the togetherness of another?

Did she herself understand it?

Mani looked at her deeply, and felt a tenderness which made him want to hug and comfort something that was throbbing with hurt.

'Maybe I am not destined to marry?' he had said then.

For a moment, her eyes had shone radiantly. But the next moment, she had hastened to say, 'Don't be silly. Shouldn't you also settle down? Shouldn't I see that and rejoice?'

Was it her eyes that spoke the truth or her tongue? Both were true.

She had slept peacefully that night.

After that, Gayathri did not seriously look out for an alliance for her son. Once in a while, a proposal would come their way, but nothing would come of it. It was difficult to say who was responsible for letting go of the opportunity – the mother or the son. The mother played her part, moved by a nameless emotion; the son completed it by fully understanding her. That was all.

'I keep looking out for good girls, Mani.'

'I know, Amma.'

'Nothing really clicks.'

'So what is the hurry?'

'That's true. Nowadays, people marry even in their thirties. Somewhere, your bride would already have been born.'

'Don't worry, Amma.'

'I don't know. If the girl who should grace this house comes, I will hand you and all my responsibilities over to her and set out without a care for a tour of the temples.'

He would look with compassion at the faultless face, which was a perverse hotchpotch of the nine emotions; at the pathetic face, on which youth and beauty lingered obstinately.

'Mahakali – the goddess of sacrifice! I have only one life to offer at your feet and pacify you!' He felt like crying with love and pain.

The years rolled by.

The mother would mechanically ask if he did not feel alone since he was unmarried and the son would reply that he did not. That was the end of it.

'Dear, are you happy?' she would sometimes ask anxiously, stroking his head.

'Of course I am.'

'There is no regret that you are not married?'

'No. I am not interested.'

A smile would spread over her face. It would vanish in a moment.

'I am a sinner. I have failed in my duty. You have gone grey.'

'Let it be.'

'It is just two of us here at home.'

'Yes.' Mani would say softly patting her with his left hand.

'But you said that that is what you like, right?'

'Yes, Amma.'

'Am I a wicked person, dear?' A deep anxiety bubbled in the inner chambers of her eyes.

'No, Amma. You are good. There is no one as good as you in the whole world.'

He lent meaning to her life.

With his left hand, Mani moved back the few grey strands that had strayed by mistake into her youthful appearance.

The darkness was giving way to dawn.

He had taken the milk that had been stored within water overnight, and heated it on the stove. Adding the coffee powder, he made coffee for his mother and himself. This was his morning routine.

'You're doing all this for me like a daughter.'

'So what?'

'Your wife should be doing this for you. Instead, you are doing this for this old woman.'

He was silent.

'Even now it is not too late. You're only forty-two, not too old for a man. Marry someone if you want to.'

Did it occur to her that at forty-two, she had to look

out for a bride for her son…What was the meaning of that glimmer in her eyes?

'No such wish, Amma.'

'No regret?'

'No.'

'Really?'

The clock sounded in the hall, and one could hear the sound of slippers at the door. Ranganathan entered.

'I am very sorry. It got late. My grandson fell down and there was a huge ruckus.' He was out of breath. He had just one daughter and this was her son.

'Did he get hurt or something?' asked Gayathri.

'Thank god not much, it was just a scratch. But the child got scared.'

'Poor thing! He is just a small child. How old is he?'

'Three.' Just as Ranganathan was answering her, the little one came running in.

'Thaatha!'

Mani stood up abruptly.

'Why did you bring the child to work?' He had instructed Ranganathan not to bring the child home.

'Don't be angry, sir. When he stopped crying, he held on to me adamantly and insisted that he would come with me. I had no option but to bring him. I will start the cooking and drop him back and return.' Ranganathan hurriedly picked up the child.

'Have you ever brought the child here before?' Gayathri asked him.

'Never, Amma. I wouldn't take such liberties. This is the first time and that, too, because of what happened…'

'It's not that. The child looks familiar, that is why I asked.'

'No, I have not brought him earlier.'

'He has lively good looks. Your daughter must also be like this. How is she?'

'She is fine, your blessings.' He started to leave the room with the child.

'Go leave him at home and then start your cooking,' Mani said.

'Why do you chase the child away? Let him be here,' Gayathri chided her son and asked Ranganathan to wait a minute.

The cook stayed on. Gayathri took a banana from the two lying on her bedside table.

'Come, little one. You like a'nana right?'

Ranganathan had no option but to go close. Mani realized that he had to step in now.

'I will give it, Amma'

He took the fruit from his mother.

Then he gave it to the child, standing between his mother and the child.

She could not see the child nor that the child took the fruit with his left hand.

Ranganathan hurried out with the child.

Mani came back and sat on the chair next to his mother.

'You didn't answer, dear.' She looked at him eagerly.

'Answer what, Amma?'

'Do you really not have any regret about not marrying, having a life of your own, a family? Really?'

'I have no such regret…no such wish.'

'Maybe after I die…'

'Even after you die, I belong to you alone, Amma. I am satisfied with being your son. Haven't I told you this many times? You are my everything.' Mani looked at her tenderly.

The summit of her triumph burned like burnished gold with his total surrender. With throbbing emotion, she picked up his hand and held it to her cheek, and that tremor ran through her whole frame.

'You are such a good child. I can be born a million times to have you as my son.' These artificial words came from the genuine fullness of her heart. The mother smiled.

Her eyes lit up.

He lived for this.

He rejoiced in this.

fourteen

The Raised Finger

WHEN NIRMALA CAME OUT after showing the outhouse to the new maid and her father, they followed her. But the little girl remained inside, staring with her eyes wide open.

'Vasanta, come out. The new Amma will get angry.'

'There is a bathroom here!'

'Come, come.'

It was an eight-square-foot room. On either side were two small rooms – one a kitchen, the other a bathroom. In the corner of the bathroom there was the toilet. This small outhouse was within the compound of the bungalow.

'You can stay here. All the three rooms have an electric connection, but if the bulbs fuse, it's you who have to replace them. You don't have to pay the electricity bill or anything,' Nirmala told them.

Her friend in the Ladies' Club had recommended Anjugam.

'A very good person, very honest. She has a daughter, Vasanta, eight years old. After her husband died, Anjugam returned to her village and stayed with her brother. As it is, her father was an unwanted burden there. Though Anjugam worked tirelessly helping her brother in the fields and his wife at home, it was impossible to bear her sister-in-law's cruel words. So she moved to Chennai with her daughter, hoping to earn a living by doing household work. She found some work in a house in Adyar, where she was permitted to stay. But there were many members in the family, including an invalid elderly lady, so they did not let her daughter stay with her. She sent Vasanta to work in a house in Nungambakkam, where she had to look after an infant. I think they fed and took care of her quite well. But for some reason, the girl did not like it there. I think she too did not like to be away from her daughter. She brought her father from the village. I think the plan is for the three of them to live together and for her to work. I have known her from the time her husband was alive. She asked me to suggest a good place for her to work in, and you too wanted some household help...'

On the fourth day, all three arrived at Nirmala's doorstep. Nagasami, about sixty-five years old, had a salt-and-pepper moustache that was incongruously stiff. Anjugam said she was thirty-five. She was of average height, with a wheatish complexion and shining teeth. But she did not smile much.

The young Vasanta was fair ('Like her father,' said Anjugam), but her growth and height had not kept pace with her eight years. She, a mere child made to babysit another

160

child! Her eyes roamed all around, as though they would swallow the world they saw. She wore a faded blue dress. She wore her thin hair in two plaits, just as she liked.

'So, all fine? You agree to work here?'

'Yes, Amma.'

Nirmala's husband, Jayakumar, was a doctor; his nursing home was three streets away. Anjugam had to go there and sweep, mop and clean the rooms. Then she had to work here, in the house. Nagasami volunteered to water the garden and maintain it. Their salary was also fixed.

'So Vasanta, what are *you* going to do?' Nirmala laughed.

Vasanta did not reply. Her lively eyes looked down.

'She will do all the household work if you guide her, Amma. Even in the other house, she would sweep the floor and draw kolam, when necessary.'

'No need. At this age, she must study. What do you say, Vasanta, will you study?'

Silence.

'Tell me. If I put you in a school, will you study?'

Still no answer.

'Why don't you answer? Amma is asking *you*...'

She did not look up, but nodded. 'Hmm.'

'Let me see. I will enquire at the Corporation school.'

Vasanta edged closer to her mother and murmured something.

'What is that? Anything about the school?'

'No, Amma...' dragged Anjugam, and then with irritation, she muttered to her daughter, 'If you want to go, go...Why tell me in front of Amma?'

'What *is* the matter?'

Vasanta lifted one little finger shyly without lifting her head, and at the same time, Anjugam said, 'She wants to go to the bathroom.'

Nirmala laughed aloud. The little girl ran towards the outhouse.

'Fine, Anjugam, I'll go in. The outhouse has remained closed for a few months because there has been no live-in help. That's why it is so dusty and dirty. First clear the cobwebs, and clean the floor with water. The three of you bring your stuff. You and your father can start working from tomorrow.'

'Yes, Amma.'

It was four in the evening. Nirmala had just stretched herself on the sofa after returning from the Ladies' Club.

Vasanta sat in the chair next to her with a notebook and pencil in her hand.

Through the open window, Nirmala could see the garden – the hibiscus and parijatha were in full bloom. Nagasami's green fingers.

'Have you written your lesson?'

'Yes, Amma'

'Show me…What is this? You have forgotten the "n" in "This is Murugan's house".'

Vasanta bit her nails. She smiled apologetically.

Nirmala felt sorry. The child had been helping her mother

without going to school all these years. When Anjugam had come to work here, the term for the Corporation schools had already started two months earlier. Now they would admit new students only next year. And they had said that since she was a totally uneducated child, they would admit her only in the first class, even though she was nine years old. Even this privilege was granted just because she had been recommended by the reputed 'Dr sir' in the neighbourhood.

'Okay, Nimma, she can be admitted to school next year. Until then, teach her a bit at home,' Jayakumar said.

'I had the same idea. If I could coach her in Tamil and Maths, we could try to put her in second class.'

But this child was just not interested in studies.

'Write again, Vasanta. This time, you must not make mistakes.'

'Yes.' She smiled brightly.

In these four months, she has lost her shyness and talks easily. There is a new sparkle in her eyes.

'If you learn well, I will even teach you science, and next year you can join a higher class.'

'Yes, Amma.'

Placing the notebook on the table and holding the pencil firmly, her head slanted, the tip of her tongue peeping out, she wrote 'this' in big letters.

'Good. Don't forget the "n" for Murugan.'

'Amma.'

'What?'

With a shy smile, she lifted her right index finger.

163

'Bathroom? Go and come back quickly.'

Vasanta ran to the outhouse. After she came back, the lessons went on for fifteen minutes.

'Did you write Murugan correctly? Very good. Now, what is this? You have written "huse" for "house"! What is this, Vasanta? Why this carelessness?'

'I'll write properly now, Amma.'

Jayakumar returned from his nursing home and got off the car.

'My head was splitting so I came back. I have to go back at five-thirty. Will you give me some tea, Nimma? I'll lie down for a while.'

'Okay…' Nirmala went in. When she returned with the tea, Jayakumar was sitting on the sofa, his head bent back. Vasanta was nowhere to be seen.

'Here, your tea. Where is Vasanta? She was writing her lessons.'

'She said she wanted to go to the bathroom.'

'What is this, Kumar? She did it just fifteen minutes ago.'

Vasanta returned and picked up the pencil and notebook. Her hair was now thicker than before, some strands floating on her forehead. With the tip of her tongue peeping out, she continued with her lessons.

'See now, Amma!'

A cry of delight. She had written the whole sentence correctly. Nirmala was looking at her curiously, and forgot to appreciate her.

Nirmala woke up at midnight. As she could not go back to sleep immediately, random thoughts flitted through her mind. *The work to be done at the Ladies' Club, sweets to be prepared next week for the silver jubilee celebration of the orphanage. Instead of regretting that they had no children of their own, Nirmala and Jayakumar had literally adopted that orphanage. Jayakumar gave the orphans free medical aid. Next week, his eldest sister was coming from Bombay. She would be happy if Nirmala took her to Mylapore to watch her favourite actor's Tamil movies. Her mother was unwell – the usual knee pain, with a headache and slight fever. Jayakumar had given her medicines. Nirmala must go and see her.*

Feeling thirsty, she got up silently without waking up her husband. When she went towards the window, the sweet scent of the night jasmine crept up her nostrils. She could see the outhouse through the window. The light was on in the bathroom and as she looked on, it went off.

She drank some water and went back to her bed. It was an hour before she could sleep. Within that time, she noticed that the light of the bathroom in the outhouse went on and off thrice.

In the morning, she saw Anjugam sweeping the hall.

'Anjugam, didn't you sleep last night?'

'I did, Amma. I went to bed last night and woke up only at five in the morning.'

'What about your father?'

'He has been sleeping well since he has come here. In my brother's house, he would cry all night, unable to bear the sharp words. Here, he is surrounded by love and he sleeps soundly. Mostly he does not even wake up in the night.'

Then it must have been Vasanta.

'Does Vasanta have a tummy upset? Or diarrhoea?'

'No, Amma. Why do you ask?'

'She looked a bit dull. I thought it must be a stomach upset. Have you swept the porch?'

It must have been her going to pee thrice in one hour. This was what she saw. God knows how many times before that and after. She does the same thing during the day. How many times has she raised her finger during lessons?

Why?

'Maybe some urinary infection. I will do some tests. How long has she had this?' asked Jayakumar when she told him about Vasanta.

'I don't know.'

'Ask her. We will also test for diabetes. Does she feel thirsty frequently? Her bladder may have become weak because of some problem and lost its power to retain urine.'

She asked Anjugam.

'Your daughter goes to the bathroom to pee very often. I noticed it and that is why I'm asking you. Please don't misunderstand me.'

'What is there to misunderstand, Amma?'

'If this continues, it will be a problem for her. Poor thing, has it been like this right from birth?'

'No.'

'Then?'

'Only...recently.'

'Does she drink too much water?'

'No.'

'You know, sir is a doctor. He says we can test her and treat her for it.'

'No-no, no need. Nothing wrong with Vasanta. This is a recent habit. She will be okay.' Anjugam said hastily.

'This is not good for her. Let sir do the tests.'

The next time she came to study, Vasanta raised the lone finger in ten minutes.

'What is this, Vasanta? Couldn't you have gone to the bathroom before we started the lessons? Okay, go. Come soon.'

She came back without delay, but raised her finger after fifteen minutes. Nirmala was slightly annoyed.

'Look here, Vasanta. If you keep running to the bathroom, you cannot study. If you don't want to study, it is okay. We will stop. Get up and go.'

'No, Amma. I want to study. I want to go to school. Now I never forget to write "n". I'll just rush to the bathroom and come back.'

'If you keep going to the bathroom like this, it is wrong. Do you know that?'

In a moment the girl's face went pale and the darting eyes stared at her.

'Will you beat me?'

Nirmala was shocked.

At once, she stroked the girl's head gently.

'Che che, why are you so scared? What is this? Will I ever hit you? I like you so much. Go to the bathroom as often as you want. We will study after you return. Sir will give you medicines to treat you.'

No diabetes, no problem with her bladder, no infection of any sort. As he held the results of her urine and blood tests in his hand, Jayakumar could not figure out the problem and was puzzled.

'Could it be some psychological problem? Nimma, do you notice anything in her behaviour?' he asked his wife at night.

'No, Kumar. Only one day, I thought her reaction was strange.'

'What was that?'

'I asked her if it was not wrong that she should go to the bathroom so often. Totally scared, she asked me if I would hit her. That was strange.'

'Maybe the people for whom she worked previously hit her. And she may have developed this problem as a consequence.'

'Could something like that happen?'

'I can't understand. But the human mind is beyond comprehension. In any case, she will become weak if this condition persists. Thank god, Akka is coming soon and it is a good thing she is a psychiatrist. We can ask her to talk to Vasanta and check if there is some suppressed fear.'

'But poor thing, she is coming here for some rest.'

'What if she is? She is a doctor, how can she refuse to help? By the way, did you visit your mother?'

'I did. She is fine now.'

'Good.'

The next day, both of them spoke to Anjugam.

'Anjugam, did the people in the house where Vasanta worked last treat her well?'

'They did, sir.'

'Did they feed her well?'

'Two full meals, a good breakfast, tea morning and evening. Can't complain.'

'Were they kind to her?'

'Yes, sir.'

'Yet she did not want to continue there?' Nirmala remembered the words of her friend at the Ladies Club.

'Nothing, Amma. It is just that she did not like being away from me,' Anjugam said with some hesitation.

'Had they ever hit her?'

Anjugam was shaken for a moment.

'Nothing like that, Amma,' she gathered herself and said in a low voice.

'Nothing like that? Then that's fine. Now we have to check on this frequent urination. It is not good for her health. And it is also a trouble for her.'

'No, Doctor sir. It is no trouble, it is just a habit. She is just a young girl, she will get over it. She is very happy here. And at peace.'

'What does that mean?'

'Mmm...only that nothing is wrong with her, she is fine. My Vasanta is fine.'

169

The night was dark and drenched in the fragrance of flowers.

Anjugam was lying down in the outhouse. Sleep eluded her. Her mind was replaying her conversation with Ayya and Amma earlier in the day.

'*Had they ever hit her?*' Where had this question come from?

Nagasami was snoring in the corner. Vasanta switched off the bathroom light and came back to lie down next to her mother, as usual. Anjugam immediately turned over to her side and stroked her daughter's head and face. She hugged her, putting her arms around her shoulders.

My child. My little one. How she had suffered in the other house! Had it been enough to feed her well? It had not been a strain for her to carry the infant – they had not pressurized her. They had even told her she could leave the baby in the cradle since her hands might ache.

But…

At night, the lady would lock the front and back doors. After the Tamil news on TV, she would go to the bedroom with her husband and the baby, and they would shut themselves in. On the floor just outside was Vasanta's bed – a mat, a pillow and a sheet.

The servants' toilet was in the backyard. If Vasanta went to the toilet at eight at night, she could go again only in the morning, when the lady woke up and opened the back door.

The little one's bladder would be full. But the servants had to suffer the torture of never being allowed to use the toilet in the house, not even in an emergency.

170

'Amma, please open the back door... I want to pee.' The small hands would knock on the bedroom door.

'Don't disturb my sleep. I can't get up now. Just control it.'

'Amma... Amma.'

'Shut up and sleep.'

The child trying to control her urge and suffering, the child growing petrified as night drew near, the child feeling scared to drink water, the little child shivering in the faded frock.

Once, just once, nature got the better of her.

Breaching her efforts to control herself, it poured on her frock, down her legs and on the floor.

'Wretched pig, dirty girl, peeing in the living room?'

Hard blows on the little cheeks and back.

'Amma, I didn't do it on purpose... Don't hit me... I couldn't control it any more...'

'Shut up...'

Vasanta stood there, humiliated, ashamed, distressed, holding her cheek and her stomach, as her tears mixed with her perspiration and ran down to join the wet pool on the floor.

'Clean the floor first with disinfectant. Dirty girl... little slut.'

When her mother came from Adyar to see her next, the little girl howled her heart out.

'I won't stay here, Ma... It is so terrible. Let us go somewhere else. It poured near the mat. I did not do it on purpose. I could not control it. I tried for a long time... I couldn't. They hit me, Ma... It hurt so much.'

'My darling.' Anjugam trembled.

'Don't tell anyone. If anyone knows that they hit me for this,

they will all make fun of me...call me dirty girl.'

Anjugam held the child to her heart.

Recalling that today, she hugged the child again.

My child, my little one...As soon as she came here, she was delighted that there was a toilet and she could go there any time. She is celebrating that. She is savouring the freedom of being able to pee when she wants to. Does she really need to go? No. Most of the time she just goes in and comes out. It is the sheer joy of being able to do that. She will stop gradually. Why does she need a doctor or medicine?

After coming to this place, that old pressure has lifted from the child. Peace and laughter have returned, she is gaining weight...her hair is growing again.

She gently kissed the child's forehead.

'Amma.'

'Yes, my dear.'

'I want to pee.'

'Go ahead.'

Vasanta ran to the toilet, and the light went on.

'Akka may be able to find out what is wrong,' Jayakumar was telling his wife.

fifteen

Threads of Emptiness

IT WAS ELEVEN WHEN I removed all the jewels from the deity in the temple and locked them securely in a box, which I placed inside the safe room. Then I locked the temple and walked down the street. Home was half a mile away on a street in Purasawakkam. It was cool and the leisurely night walk relaxed my body and mind. Was that right? How could the pleasant air outside relax the mind?

Of late, I had no mental peace. If the priest who offered daily prayers at the temple lost his peace of mind, then what could be the remedy? The mere proximity of the deity used to give me joy in the past. Now there was unrest and doubt, and no faith. Did I deserve to continue to do this work, just because I wore the panchakachcham, tiruneer and rudraksham? The day I had stood in the sanctum without peace in my heart, I had ceased to be a believer.

I reached home. Even before I knocked on the door, the

latch within was unfastened. Muktha stood there. In the dim light of the 25-watt lamp, her face glowed with pure unalloyed beauty.

'Wash your feet and come, Appa. I will serve the food.'

'It is too late. I don't feel hungry. Just give me some buttermilk.'

'Appa, at least have some rasam sadam, and then butter milk. Otherwise, you will feel hungry in the middle of the night. So what if it is late now?'

'Just get on with it – finish eating and go to bed. A nice duo, father and daughter…' That was my wife calling out sleepily from the corner of the room. Toiling all day long, the non-stop chores had exhausted her. This disruption of her sleep past eleven must be an annoyance. I bolted the door and switched off the light. The green night light on the wall struggled for a moment in the sudden darkness, then shone steadily. I tiptoed to the kitchen behind Muktha.

I watched her hand as she poured out the rasam. It was like ivory, and well rounded, though it belonged to the daughter of a poor temple priest. The carefree joy with which she had played around here as my child before her marriage had nourished it. Now the ivory had dimmed.

Her fingers were wrapped around the rasam ladle and were not open. Thank goodness…

I wiped my mouth with the cloth on my shoulders after washing my hands. 'Sambho Mahadeva.' My mouth uttered the name out of sheer habit, and then a burp too came on its own after the meal.

174

'Muktha, go to sleep. I can't sleep now. I will sit outside for a while.'

I went out, stepping into the dimness of the night light. I rested my head on my arms as I lay on the cot and closed my eyes. Red streams went down my visual screen. Formless scenes, sights I had seen every day and faces – Lingam, Amman…and then all of them would be erased. Muktha, lean and pale, beauty in a line drawing. She used to talk a lot then, and laugh. Not any more. Now she spoke only when necessary and smiled formally, and even then the smile remained on her lips, it did not reach her eyes.

I noticed this change more after she came from her husband's house in a village near Tiruchi. She did not explain why. Her silence was more eloquent.

Black demons crowded in my eyes. Who was that near my feet? Startled, I opened my eyes. Hadn't she slept?

'What is this, Muktha? It is going to be midnight. Why are you sitting here and not sleeping?'

'I feel protected, Appa, when I am with you.'

Anguish sliced my heart. *What was she saying? What was this fear looming over her? Shall I give her some vibhuti? 'Thedarkiniya seeralikkum sivayanama enritum neerey.' (The ash on the forehead and the words Shivayanama bestow grace rare to find.) A mechanical recital…In these Bhakti poems, there is poetry and there is bhakti, but underneath that is there truth?…Meaningless words.*

Faith is god, they say. Then it is our belief which creates Him, isn't it? If the thinker creates the thought, then the thought has

175

no separate existence. If it has a separate existence, then should everyone's perception of it not be alike? My daughter is afraid. Seeing this, I am tormented. This alone is Truth. God has no place here.

'It is getting late, Amma. Let us go in.' I rose.

It was a little late when I woke up in the morning. I brushed my teeth hurriedly. When I came to the central room, I noticed the room opposite. It was the poojai room, which used to be resplendent with pictures of swamis, lamps and flowers. My grandsons, one seven years old and one five, were standing there with eyes closed and hands folded. They had had a bath, and with vibhuti (sacred ash) shining on their foreheads and an expression of concentration, their moist lips recited from *Sivanandalahari*: '*Trayi vedyam hrudyam tripuraharam aadyam trinayanam*' (He who is known by the Three Vedas, who delights the heart, who destroyed Tripura, who is the primordial one, who is three-eyed). Then they chanted from *Thevaram*: '*Pitha piraisoodi perumaane arulaala*' (O Mad One! Wearing the crescent, Oh lord who gives his grace).

They opened their eyes and prostrated themselves on the floor. They were pleased with themselves and their mother smiled at them, after which they came out. I saw that she – my daughter-in-law – was looking at the pictures thoughtfully.

'Thaatha, we have said the slokams and done the namaskarams.'

'Good,' I said, looking at their smiling faces.

'We are good boys, no Thaatha?'

'Of course you are, my darlings.'

'Thaatha, there is this Suresh, in our class. He is very bad. He never says his prayers. He says there is no god and even makes fun of our vibuthi. He will surely go to hell, no Thaatha?' asked the older one.

Where is this boy's father now? In heaven or hell? Where do vibrant young men who fight with a thief on a running train, to be pushed to death by him, go? He believed in god too. He too said his prayers every day, like these boys. I was the one who taught him that. If I had instead taught him how to save himself from a thief…?

'Tell me, Thaatha. He will surely go to hell, no?'

'We must never condemn anyone to hell, Kanna.'

'Bad people will go to hell. He is a bad boy. Only those who believe in god are good. Good things will happen only to them. God will punish those who do not believe in Him.'

He had such faith and such trust. I too was like him once. Why had I changed? I had not taught them to pray and worship like I had taught my son. But it was not just that; even when my wife taught them I looked on like an impersonal spectator.

The two boys stood before me, symbols of piety, wearing vibhuti and with an earnest glow on their faces.

For a minute I longed for that complete trust which a child is capable of. That would have been a protection. 'I feel protected, Appa, when I am with you.' My body shivered… Why did she say that?

No. I don't want that childish certainty and I won't have it either. When we are children, we learn certain values from our

177

elders. In the course of our life, they change, they must change. Change is the fact of life. With our life experiences, those values either become firm or disappear. They cannot remain the ready-made values with which we were brought up. If they do, then it means that the mind of the person has not evolved. Life is wasted on such a person.

'Thaatha, I am right, no? God exists, no?'

'If you keep talking about this, you will get late for school. Is there any homework you have left unfinished?'

As soon as they left, my wife came in, fuming with anger.

'I was listening to all that and I want to know. What has happened to you? If the children really want to know something, can't you reply properly?'

'What should I say? Tell me. If they ask me does god exist, how do I know?'

'Siva, Siva…what is this heresy and that too from a temple priest? It is bhakti and poojai which give solace during all the grief. And you…'

She stopped. Our eyes turned to the same place – the poojai room. There, our daughter-in-law was handing over the naivedyam tray to Muktha. And Muktha received it with reverence, with both hands. She had opened her hands now and my whole body trembled involuntarily when I saw the white marks left by deep burns. The day she came home, Muktha had told us that one day while cooking in her husband's house, she had absent-mindedly held the utensil, forgetting that it would be hot, and had got deep burns on her hands.

'Look at her hands. This was a real escape from death. She escaped by a hair's breadth. If the sari had caught fire…Thank god, by His grace that did not happen and only her hands got burnt. Otherwise, we would have lost our daughter as we lost our son…What is the sense in giving lectures about there being no god?' my wife said in a choked voice.

'It is getting late. I will go for my bath.' I rushed inside. The others had bathed long ago. My grandsons had gone to school. My daughter-in-law was a teacher in the Corporation school and when she left for work, Muktha stood at the door, watching her walk away.

After my bath, I applied the tiruneer out of sheer habit. In the same way, I performed the evening poojai. My heart accused me: 'Liar, liar.'

A car drove up to the front door and my wife turned to me.

'The banker's driver has come. It seems they have come to the temple. They have asked you to go in the car with the temple keys.'

Whatever the job may be, should I not be dedicated to it as long as I work? I got ready and rushed out, feeling guilty about neglecting my duty.

'You haven't eaten anything.'

'It is late. I will eat in the afternoon.'

'I can't understand why you woke up so unusually late. What will the 'big people' waiting for you at the temple think if the priest is late and the temple is still locked?'

The driver gave me a scornful smile and opened the door.

He started the car. He had come to take me only because he was bound to obey his employer, otherwise he belonged to the group that smashed Pillayar idols. When we turned into the street with the temple, he coughed and spat with contempt. He seemed pleased at insulting god. He was certain there was a god for him to insult. But me? What right did I have to serve as a priest when I saw only an omnipresent void?

The car halted and I got down hurriedly.

'Come, come Gurukkal. Why so late? Did you go to sleep late?' The bank officer winked at me. His wife, who stood next to him, grimaced with discomfort. Next to them were their two young sons and a daughter.

I opened the temple and went in. There was no one else but this family. I quickly started decorating the Amman with the jewels. *'Nana ratna vichitra bhooshanakari'* (One who is adorned with exquisite jewels and precious stones) – a lovely turn of phrase.

'When there are so many burning social issues, why did he choose this for his research…?' One of the sons was criticizing some professor's writing. It was obviously a continuation of an earlier discussion.

'Why, isn't dowry a social issue?' His brother.

'That's an old issue. Now the practice has come down drastically. I'm not going to accept dowry when I marry; nor will my friends. Nor are we going to give dowry for Leela. The problem is not relevant any more. What is the point in flogging a dead horse, like the dowry issue? It would have been more useful if he had done some research and written about something political and sociological about humankind, like racial violence.'

'The other day I read an article that said – women are more susceptible to jealousy than men. I was annoyed.' The daughter.

'Why get annoyed? It's true. Not just being jealous…if a woman decides to be wicked, the man's life becomes a hell. The woman uses her charm and entices and ensnares the man. She fleeces him for her own welfare and protection. Only status and ostentation are important to her. If he wants to read a book or enjoy nature, she wants to go to the Ladies Club dressed in all her finery and play rummy, while bragging about her husband's achievements. All she cares for are material values. It's a rare woman who really understands her husband.'

'Did you recently read a book written by a western author? Or are you saying this on the basis of a friend's experience?' The daughter laughed and her brother's face turned red.

'You may say anything, Leela, but the poor man is nothing before the destructive power of the woman. All this talk of suffering women has no basis in today's reality.'

Is he right? Has equality between man and woman been achieved completely? I too have seen the wickedness of woman in some families. Does the truth, as usual, lie somewhere in between – neither this end, nor that? It is wrong, in fact, to refer to truth in the singular…it is really truths. Each one's experience is their truth. There are as many truths as there are people in this world. Can we deny this?

If the woman is not weak, then I need not worry about Muktha, isn't it? But her exhaustion? The eyes that have forgotten how to smile weigh heavily on my heart.

What is this? Are these my hands doing the poojai with the flowers? When did I decorate the Amman? When did I start? The banker's family is standing there looking at the deity with reverence, and the devotees have gathered and I, the priest, am reciting the mantrams... My mind has registered all this only now. Che! Can performing a ritual so mechanically, as though in a dream while the mind is elsewhere, be called poojai? I am not fair to myself, nor am I fair to god, if there is such a thing.

'Gurukkal Aiya, I want an abhishekam to be done.'

By now a big crowd had gathered.

It was two when I returned home for lunch. I lay down on the bench as I was tired. My eyes were burning because I had not slept the night before. The sleep I had got in the early hours of the morning was not enough to revive my spirits. It would be good to get a few winks. But my closed eyes could not sleep.

'Are you sleeping?'

'Yes, I am. And I am talking in my sleep,' I snapped at my wife and glared at her.

'Please don't get angry.' She sat down and heaved a sigh.

'I wanted to tell you something. But I did not want to disturb you in case you were asleep. That's why I asked.'

'Oh! You shouted in my ears because you did not want to wake me up, is it?'

'Eswaraa…' she mumbled and bent down and stared at the floor. I felt sorry.

'What is it, tell me.'

'Nothing. It is now one month since Muktha came home. Should we not take her back to her husband?'

'She has lost so much weight. If she falls ill, there are not even any proper medical facilities in that village. Let her rest here for some more time.'

'One day or the other she will have to return. If we keep delaying, won't they get angry?'

'Has her husband written to her, asking her to come back?'

'Does that tight-lipped girl ever tell me anything? I asked her for how long has your husband asked you to stay here. She stares at me and says she does not know. I think there is some problem. We just have to ignore that and take her back. She is young and whatever it is, that is where she belongs.'

'So you want me to get the money ready for the train fare?'

'Not just that. Even if we do not give her jewellery and saris, we must make some sweets and send those with her.'

'Where do we get the money?'

'God will take care of that.'

'You mean as He has done till now?'

'I will leave if you are going to talk like this…And you are a great temple priest who chants His name every day!'

'I'm going to resign from this job.'

'Why?' She blinked.

'That is the right thing to do. Tomorrow itself, I'm going to meet the dharmakarthas.'

183

'What is wrong with you?' she asked in a feeble voice. What was that on her face – fear, sadness or worry?

'I do not have any peace of mind. I must not do this work with doubts and restlessness.'

'What then…for a living?'

I laughed. 'See? Even you do not see it as a lofty profession but only as a money earner. Don't worry. I am planning to get a loan from the banker to start a small shop or something.'

'I do not say I am not worried about our livelihood. We are poor people. Can we live without worrying? But since your job is one of devotion to the cause of god, it gives us some happiness and peace…That is also true.'

Many truths…Many truths that are close but in conflict with each other.

'I too felt that happiness and peace of mind long ago. God was not just a symbol that I worshipped but a truth that throbbed with a life of its own within me. I thought that I could make the whole world beautiful with that eternal beauty. But in the end…hmm…life is a big traitor.' My voice faded into the beyond.

'I understand,' she said gently, with a comforting smile, her hand on my shoulder. 'But I don't want to understand. You're upset now. Take a rest.' She went in.

I lay on my back, staring at the ceiling for a while. A shadow fell on me. Muktha.

I sat up and indicated the bench.

'Come, Muktha.'

She sat down. I looked at the eyes that had lost their smile.

How run down she looked. Was this mere exhaustion? There was a wasting, as though the root of life had been affected by a pestilence. Could it be some horrible disease? Sambho Mahadeva! Those words were just an exclamation, that's all. Merely words that conveyed surprise, sorrow, shock.

As I kept looking at her, my eyes were screened by tears.

'Appa.'

'What, Amma?'

'Amma says I should go back soon. I...I won't go, Appa.'

'That's what I told her too. Stay here and rest. You have become awfully thin. Is anything wrong with your health?'

She did not reply. She continued to sit there, her head bent down. Then she slowly opened out her fingers and showed me her hands. I looked at the white skin.

'Appa, this did not really happen because I accidentally held a hot utensil. It happened because my mother-in-law placed red-hot coals on my palms while my two sisters-in-law held my hands tight.'

The entire universe seemed to crash over me. The volcano which erupted inside me poured forth boiling lava and stopped. I realized I was wet all over with perspiration and my arms were around my child.

'What? What did you say? Blabbering, are you? Would anyone do such a thing...would anyone...? Did you have a nightmare? Muktha, what is this? Is this true?'

She was weeping silently.

'Was there no one to protest against this horror? Why didn't you tell your husband? Was he watching this?'

'It was he who handed the coals and the tongs to my mother-in-law.'

I felt a burst of salty blood on my lips. My lip had bled where I had bitten it. My heart, which throbbed like a hurricane, slowed down and the agitation subsided. Why be agitated now?

I was aware of only one thing at that time. I was certain that if my son-in-law had been there before me, I would have throttled him with my hands and killed him calmly, without a trace of doubt.

'Why did they do this?' I sounded wooden.

'My crime was that I had not woken up early enough to make the coffee as always. The previous day I had ground two measures of rice for dosai and I was totally exhausted, so I slept longer than usual. My mother-in-law abused me, accusing me of being deliberately indifferent and careless.'

'Demons!'

'That is not the real reason, but just an excuse. It seems you have not given the dowry that was promised. You have not been giving them kitchen utensils, jewellery and so on for each festival. It seems they did not think we would be so abysmally poor. For so many days, they harassed me verbally. They made me work like a beast of burden. I would have put up with all that had my husband shown love. They did this as a warning and sent me here. I was given strict orders not to tell you what had happened. They think that out of fear that this would be repeated, I would make sure that you sent me back with loads of gifts.'

I wanted to laugh aloud for in my mind I heard that young man's voice saying: 'The problem is not relevant any more. What is the point in flogging a dead horse, like the dowry issue?…It is not correct to say now that women are suffering.' *How easily he had passed a judgement on the basis of a few instances. It was his youth. At his age, how would he know that there are many truths?*

Was it possible for him, a person used to a rich urban lifestyle, to understand our society? What he saw was a truth, but a miniscule truth. What I had heard just now was the more prevalent truth.

My child…Live coals placed deliberately on her skin… God…the word fell like a dry leaf. This was the perfect emptiness. A destruction akin to death. What was left thereafter?

'Appa.'

'What, Amma?' I could not hear my own voice.

'If I go there again, I do not think I will come back alive.'

'Muktha.'

'I don't want to go there. Not just now…ever again.'

I shut my eyes. This horror, this fear, this degradation…the viciousness that was the genesis of it all.

What is the remedy? Human compassion, help, love. What else do you need?

I had a dream. I too had a dream, like an inheritance…a beautiful dream. You were the fragrance of that dream. Do you remember that god? When did you leave? But there was a lingering fragrance in the space vacated by you…The fragrance of 'I' after the fragrance of 'You'. My doubts, my metamorphosis, my rejection – these were the sweet smells of the towering 'I'. I stood in darkness. I stood alone. I stand before the question mark that is the world. Henceforth, if I say 'God', it is a name for this courage.

I opened my eyes. 'Don't worry, Muktha. You need not go there. We will somehow overcome this. The world has not come to an end.'

sixteen

The Wife of a Genius

THE TWO MEN WHO WERE TALKING to each other in soft voices stopped when the lady entered the room. They stood up.

'Vanakkam.'

'Namaskaram. Please sit down.'

The two men would have been forty-five and fifty. Both were dressed similarly, in a shirt and veshti, wore thick black-rimmed glasses, and had a sandalwood streak on their foreheads. One had a leather bag in his hand. He spoke.

'I am Ezhilvendan, the secretary of the celebration committee. This is Thiru Ranganathan – in charge of the souvenir.'

The lady nodded without saying anything.

'We had already written to you about all this. Your grand-daughter told us that we could meet you today.'

'Hmm.'

'The world of Carnatic music is indebted to Thiru

Panchanadam. Music lovers will treasure any details they can gather on him.'

'Not just them. Other singers, reviewers, and people like us connected to music concerts – no one knows anything about his life. So these details will be a real boon,' added Ranganathan.

The visitors were uncomfortable as nothing was forthcoming from the old lady, except 'hmm'. Did they have to extract information from her? Where had the young girl who had asked them to come in disappeared? It was she who had written to them and welcomed them, saying she would tell her Paatti that they had come.

'We were very disappointed when you refused to meet us initially. We were much relieved after we got your consent,' said Ezhilvendan.

'But…but even now, I do not think I can help you.' The lips did not appear to move on that expressionless face.

The visitors were startled, and it was Ezhilvendan who gathered himself first.

'We cannot understand why you say so. What objection can you have to giving us the information? We are a very old society, a highly respected one, which has been organizing music concerts.'

A streak of a smile ran across the woman's face.

'Sarada Sangita Nilayam is celebrating its diamond jubilee. Even if I cannot sing, I belong to this district, Tanjavur, where music flows like the Kaveri. And I also shared my life with a musician. Wouldn't I know about your Nilayam at least by that association? You don't have to introduce yourself to me at all.'

'Sorry for selling needles in a blacksmiths' street! When you have such a good opinion of us, why shouldn't you cooperate with us?'

'Have you any doubts about the souvenir?' Ranganathan stepped into the conversation. 'It will have interviews of the great masters, articles and memoirs. If you want to assure yourself of the quality...' He opened the leather bag, taking it from Ezilvendan.

'Don't trouble yourself. I've no doubt about its excellence. My regret is that I do not have anything like the details you want.'

The two men looked with surprise in the direction of the frail voice. Could a frail voice convey such firmness? Could a thin, aged frame be so adamant?

With tranquillity, Gowri Ammal took in those stares, which combined surprise and a little annoyance. Now past sixty, her frame was devoid of flesh, though she had not become bony. Age had drawn a few wrinkles on her wheatish skin. The eyes behind the cataract spectacles, which were thick like soda glasses, looked extra large and stared at them. But her expression was not stern. The tranquillity conveyed a kind of detachment, and not peace. There was no kumkum on her forehead, which was smeared with vibhuti, the holy ash. It must have been years since she had removed her nose rings, but the marks of the closed holes could be seen on both sides of her nose.

191

The impression of softness that her appearance gave was the result of her age. Even in her youth, she could not have been good-looking.

Wondering how to make some headway with her, the two men were greatly relieved when they saw Bhuvana entering the room. They felt infused with new hope.

She brought two cups of coffee on a tray, which she placed on a stool before them.

'I went to the kitchen to make coffee after telling Paatti that you had come. That is why I did not join you. I'm very sorry.' The beautiful young girl would have been seventeen or eighteen. She continued, 'Have you spoken to Paatti? Ever since you wrote to her, it is I who has been so excited, more than Paatti.' She sat down on a chair that was a little away from them.

'It looks as if your Paatti is not very interested in the idea.'

'What is this? I argued with her so much and got her permission. Would she have agreed if she wasn't interested?'

This beauty had certainly not been inherited from the grandmother. They recalled a faded old photo they had seen. The picture showed a man with a radiant face, a knot of hair, sacred ash on his forehead, earrings, a high-necked coat and an angavastram, in keeping with the fashion of older times, and the natural good looks were evident. Panchanadam, with his wide forehead, bright and smiling eyes, nose that gave him a Greek profile, and sculpted lips and chin, must have been thirty years old then. The radiance and loveliness of this girl had its genesis there.

Ezhilvendan brushed his thoughts aside and addressed her with an ingratiating smile, 'I don't know about that. It is now your responsibility to get your Paatti's permission.'

'What is this, Paatti? What is your problem with telling them details about Thaatha? We will be so proud if it is published in the souvenir!'

Gowri said nothing.

About two weeks ago, she had received a letter from Sarada Sangita Nilayam in Tiruvallikeni. This organization of great standing, which had nobly served the cause of music, musicians and instrumentalists for sixty years, would be holding a grand celebration of its diamond jubilee in three months. On the occasion, they intended to release a souvenir containing interesting details about and life sketches of great musicians.

Panchanadam was one of the important singers of yester-years. He was a genius who had died at the age of thirty-two. Not only was he a great singer, but he had also composed many devotional songs in Sanskrit and Tamil. Some critics were of the opinion that his compositions were unparalleled when it came to expressing the soul of some rare ragas. He had even created a new raga. So those compiling the souvenir were desirous of publishing his personal details and had written to Gowri Ammal. She had responded in the negative. But Bhuvana, who was with her, was keen that her grandfather should feature in this prestigious publication and had persuaded her grandmother to agree.

'After having said yes, Paatti, how can you now keep quiet?'

Gowri Ammal looked at the visitors before her.

'You must not misunderstand me. I asked you to come in person only to convince you that I had nothing to say and also because my granddaughter pestered me. In fact, I even asked her to write to you not to come here with too much hope. Bhuvana, didn't you do that?'

'She did write that. But we are quite surprised that you have no information.' This was Ezhilvendan.

'Information...what information? He was born in an orthodox Brahmin family in Sozhavandan, Thanjavur district in 1906. It is said that the people of Thanjavur drink the love for music along with their mother's milk. My father-in-law told me that it was so with my husband too and that he was very talented at a very young age. Unless he was blessed even in the womb, could he have composed two hundred and fifty compositions by the time he was thirty-two? He stopped studying after his school finals. We got married when he was studying in school. He was enamoured of Tiruvaiyaru, as his name indicates. He was totally devoted to Tyagabrahmam.[4] He had no other guru. He lived in Tiruvaiyaru, but he would keep visiting other places – Thiruvananthapuram one day, then here, and suddenly Erode or Pollaachi. But wherever he was, his sole focus was Carnatic music. We had one daughter...this girl's mother. When our daughter was about five years old, he fell ill with some viral fever. There were no medical facilities then. God knows what it was. He had a raging fever for four days and he died on the fifth. He was thirty-two then.'

Gowri said this as if she were reciting a lesson, without

any emotion, in an even voice bereft of tonal variations. This was a ritual. Her manner indicated that this was something that had to be endured.

Ranganathan smiled sheepishly and squirmed in his chair.

'Those…those details are already well known. We do not want this. The whole world knows what you just said, like statistics. It was nothing new.'

He stopped and took out some papers from the bag.

'Please go through this.'

Gowri Ammal shook her head with a smile.

'Why should I see it? You say so and that is enough.' She distanced herself from the subject.

But Bhuvana got up eagerly.

'Let me see.'

She took a look at the papers. Apart from the occasional special issues published by Sarada Sangita Nilayam, there was a picture of Panchanadam. It was not very clear.

'This is Thaatha! Paatti! We have the same picture, no?' she shouted gleefully, carrying the papers to the older woman.

'The same one. That's the only one we have! He was thirty then!' Gowri Ammal said without even glancing at it.

'Sir! We have the same one at home, it is framed and hung on the wall.' Echoed Bhuvana.

'Amma, you are not saying anything.' Ranganathan turned to Gowri Ammal.

'Why? I gave you all the details without even taking a breath.' Gowri Ammal's lips were tight.

'But those were well known ones…'

'Do you want the truth or some unknown details?'

It seemed as if the old woman was possessed by a mischievous sprite.

'My daughter's name is Janaki. Soon after she was married, I too settled down in Chennai. Her husband, Vanchinathan, is an advocate. She lives in Abhiramapuram and has two children. Bhuvana, the older one, is doing a pre-university course. She comes often to Egmore to see me. The other is a boy, Panchanadam, Thaatha's name. We call him Panchu. These may be details not known to you.'

The visitors tried to control their irritation. They wanted details only about the departed musician and this hag had deliberately avoided the subject…the typical cussedness of the southern part of Tamil Nadu!

It seemed as if in an instant, a screen covered Gowri Ammal's face again.

'That is okay. Now have your coffee, it is getting cold.'

Restraining themselves in deference to her age, they drank the coffee.

'These are useful too. But if you could share some personal anecdotes about him, it would be nice. That is what we want,' said Ranganathan.

'Personal details?'

'His preferences, habits, some words he used often, the way he laughed, what they call mannerisms…things like that.'

'That is to say something of human interest that readers will like…small details,' explained Ezhilvendan.

'Nothing like that,' said Gowri Ammal,

'Preferences? Habits? He was a great devotee. A devotee who worshipped beauty...that is, human beauty. And by human, I mean any body excluding men, and as for the others, anybody older than ten and younger than fifty.' Could she say this? If she did, would they accept it as a fitting answer to their question about his preferences and habits?

'Please try to remember. You are his wife, who lived with him. Who else would be capable of knowing his personal details? Even something like his favourite food...'

'It is now thirty-five years since he died. How can I remember?'

'Paatti, they are not asking for anything big. You have told me that after having his coffee in the afternoon, he would sometimes ask for a "piece of betel nut". They only want something like that.'

Ranganathan's face lit up.

'Exactly. So that means you remember some small things. Can you tell us something like that? I will note that down right away. "After coffee, he would ask for a piece of betel nut".' Murmuring the words under his breath, Ranganathan pulled out a pen and a paper from the leather bag and started writing.

Gowri laughed.

She laughed, and the laugh grew in loudness.

She laughed, rocking in the easy chair, unable to control herself.

She laughed again; her whole body shook. She removed her spectacles and wiped the tears streaming down from her eyes.

The others looked at her strangely.

Her laughter stopped as suddenly as it had started. She sat like that for a while, gasping for breath.

Then she wore her spectacles again. There was a new softness about her face. Her words resonated with an extra-ordinary strength and sweetness, as if the sound was a melody that had come alive in the heart of truth.

'He was a genius. He sang as if he was born from the veena that belonged to the goddess of music. He composed immortal works. Is it important to know if he had a cut of betel nut or betel shavings after his coffee in the afternoon? Like everyone else, he ate, he slept, he breathed, he went to the bathroom, he perspired in the heat, felt chilly in the cold, had a child, was born and later died. Are these the parameters to measure a genius? They must be assessed only by their divine moments. That is, the moments when they lived, which held true meaning. It is those radiant moments which set them apart from the rest of the world. We need not worry about the other moments.'

Even if the other moments were strung together by female forms.

No one spoke for a while. Ezhilvendan cleared his throat.

'You're right. But won't the public also be interested in the other moments?'

'Actually, ordinary people will be more interested in the other moments.' This was Ranganathan.

'Then let them read about ordinary people.'

'But people are interested because these ordinary details

are about great people. There are so many people with a beard in this world, but we talk about it only when it is Tagore.'

'If people are interested in ordinary details only because they are about a genius, it means that the focus of interest is the genius, isn't it? Why don't you let the genius remain at that height? What pleasure do you get from dragging them down to our level?'

'We would still like some human interest stories. How did he manage the tussle between giving priority to his art and his family life? Was he a good husband? What is your view as a wife? Did he write to you regularly when he was away? Do you have any of his letters? Readers will find that very interesting.' Ezhilvendan went on when Gowri Ammal cut in.

'On the one hand, you say you want to see the ordinary side of a genius. On the other hand, you do not grant a genius the privilege that you grant an ordinary person. Is that fair?'

'What do you mean?'

'Every man's personal life is a private affair. He has the right to keep it private. Your questions seem to violate that right. For example, you mentioned a letter. Isn't a letter between a husband and wife a very private one? And you want to publish that in your article?'

'Then you have a letter of his ...?' Ranganathan asked eagerly.

'That is not the point. Even if there was one, I would not give it to you. If a person is beyond the ordinary, should he lose his right to protect his privacy? Do his likes and dislikes, joys and sorrows and habits become public property? Is this a punishment for excellence? Is this how the mediocre punish the extraordinary?'

'What can we do if you misconstrue whatever we say? Forget it. Can you tell us something about the many compositions he created based on the rare ragas?'

'Must be eighty.'

'We don't want the number. Did he strain to create or did it come without effort? How was he inspired? What interested him in the rare ragas?'

'In any art, creation is the dialogue between man and god. There is no room for a third person. That being so, what would I know about the birth pangs of his creations?'

'He composed a new ragam and called it Girisutha. Can we take it that it was in praise of you?'

Gowri Ammal stared at the emptiness far away.

'No. It was not for me. He was always a devotee of the goddess.'

'That is a new point. I'll take it down…Anything else?'

'I'm sorry. Please do not take it amiss. I have nothing to tell you that will interest you. Thank you for coming all the way.'

She had indicated that they could leave.

'Fine. If you do not want to tell us anything, what else can we do? We will go. And sorry for the trouble.'

The old lady did not even make a demur for the sake of politeness.

'Paatti, you're too…' burst out Bhuvana, but Gowri Ammal

cut in.

'Bhuvana, go and see them off.'

The quiet authority in that tone silenced the others.

After sending Bhuvana to do her bidding, she went to her room and locked it on the inside. There, on the wall, hung an old-fashioned picture. The radiant face of a man wearing his hair in a knot, earrings and a high-collared coat smiled at her. He was very handsome. He was only thirty.

Gowri stared at the picture for a while. What a smile! A smile that won hearts? Is that why so many women were enchanted? Did those lips merely smile and lure women…? Those lips also sang till your heart melted…those lips…

Music, creation, Girisutha…who was the woman who had intoxicated him so much as to give birth to the raga? Had he given it that name, which indicated his wife, in jest or out of guilt?

His behaviour towards her had never indicated that he felt guilt or remorse!

How many days had she shed tears because one side of him was music and the other was betrayal! How many times had she attempted to change him and failed! Though she had burnt with jealousy and rage, she had truly believed that one day she would win him over with her true love! How she had throbbed with grief because his premature death had not only dashed her hopes and turned her into a young widow, but it had also made his betrayal immutable. Those moments were her secret hell. Whenever she thought of him, feelings of rage, unrequited love, a wife's jealousy and hatred for all those girls coursed through her, especially when she saw that letter.

It was written to some woman in Thiruvananthapuram. Somehow it had got mixed up with his belongings. After he had died, Gowri had found it among his clothes. She had preserved this letter, along with some of his other things, in his memory. It had become a habit to torture herself by looking at this item that hurt her. Whenever she saw the letter, she would feel like tearing it up. But she had still preserved it.

Gowri slowly sat down on the floor in front of the cupboard and opened the lock of the drawer at the bottom. She pulled it out and took out a small blue box. It opened with a rusty screech. The stench of age and smell of naphthalene balls assaulted her. The box was full of memorabilia, clothes he had worn, parrots made of pith from a rose garland he had worn years ago, her wedding sari, a few notebooks in which he had made some jottings for his musical creations, the pen he had used, some insipid postcards he had sent her, and that postmark-jabbed letter.

She opened it with her thin hands. The letter that shook in her quivering hands had become fragile, as if it would break into bits. She knew it by heart – how many times had she read it! The letter was brimming full of emotion and words that expressed love, passion and pain to the one who remained nameless, and was called 'Dearest' and 'Darling'. If she had given the letter to those men, claiming that it was addressed to her, they would have praised him for having been a devoted husband and happily published it. The readers would have been amply rewarded with a 'human interest' story. Smiling wryly at the thought, she read it again, as she had done hundreds of times earlier.

She finished reading it. She was surprised that unlike the other times, her insides were not ruffled by the usual storm. Where had those spears of anger and jealousy that used to tear her heart apart disappeared? Why wasn't her heart throbbing with pain? She was actually sitting peacefully!

She had thought that the hurt would never heal. How had it healed? Was time on her side?

She, with her grey hair, wrinkled skin and cataract glasses, sat in front of the youthful face. Who was the man who died thirty years ago? Was he really her husband?

He did not appear to be her husband now.

'You could be my son!' she thought curiously. And with this feeling, that young man's love and letter lost their sharpness, and shrank to become a pigmy figure before her towering presence.

seventeen

A Cleansing

Tᴜʟᴀꜱɪ ʟᴏᴏᴋᴇᴅ ᴛʜᴏᴜɢʜᴛғᴜʟʟʏ at her father. Srinivasan was doing his poojai in the worship room, his thoughts, words and deeds entwined as one in devotion. His work as the temple priest had never made him disrupt his poojai at home. Just as the child who loves sweets stretches out his hand for one more chocolate, Srinivasan never tired of the rituals of worship.

'Is the tirukkannamudhu – sweet offering for god – ready, Amma?'

'Here, Appa.'

As he offered it to god, he thought it looked 'delicious'. He was filled with a sense of both sadness and joy. Whatever Tulasi did was faultless. The kolams on the floor and in front of the altar spoke eloquently of her grace and aesthetic sense. Not surprisingly, she, who was so good and beautiful, was not blessed with good fortune. That unfortunate husband of hers had died very early, without enjoying a life together with her.

When he closed his eyes to pray, all he could think of was his daughter. But what could he pray for her? Maybe: 'you took away everything from her, at least give her peace'. But what did that mean? When there was nothing else…what did one do with peace?

He prostrated himself in obeisance.

'Tulasi. I have done the naivedyam. Come here, do your prayers and then take it away. I am leaving for the temple.'

'Yes, Appa.'

'Today there is Tirumanjanam – the ritual bath for the deity – in the temple. Will you come?'

'I have work at home.'

'Whatever you say.'

As he stepped out, Srinivasan saw the little boy hovering around. The boy slunk away as soon as he saw Srinivasan; he was here only because of Tulasi. What was the magic she wove that she had come to be so easily ensconced in that little heart? Probably to that seven- or eight-year-old orphan, anyone who showed a bit of kindness seemed like a 'mother'. They say that ether is all-pervading. Could motherhood be a subtle all-pervasive presence too? Did it flow from the source just by a touch? He did not stop that flow of love. Let her do what she wanted for that boy. But should he, Srinivasan, adopt a nameless brat as his grandson?

He was not just an orphan.

He was not just a *cheri* boy – one who lived in a colony of untouchables.

205

He was beyond the fringe of the four varnas – a *panchama* boy, belonging to the lowest caste, untouchable.

His skin was so dark that it seemed it would stain what he touched. In jest he was called 'Vellai' (white) by the people in the kuppam. No one knew his name. Vellai was well aware of his status.

'No one should touch me. If you did, you would feel a shock,' he grinned.

Srinivasan frowned. He had never considered himself very old-fashioned or inhuman. If he were, would he even allow this boy to come near his house? But there was a limit to everything…This mite, who had no father, no mother, no name and no caste, had sprung from nowhere…

But wasn't he worshipping a 'certain something' born of itself, with no father, no mother, no name and no caste, day and night, at the temple and at home; worshipping that Being with a thousand names?

Narayana, Narayana! What is this! He hastened along after shaking off that sacrilegious thought.

Tulasi called out to Vellai, who had been hiding behind the karunocchi plants, peeping out now and then. On hearing her, he rushed out.

'Vellai, come and have payasam.'

'Periyavar may come now.'

'He won't.'

'He saw me. That's why…'

His body remained taut as he spoke, his feet positioned in

readiness to run away. There was an unseemly caution and an excessive fear which did not befit a child of his years. Did this tragedy not affect Appa at all?

'Tulasi, there are countless orphans. Don't I feel pity and compassion for them? But should we bring one of those creatures right into this house?'

Her head heard the arguments, but her heart had travelled far beyond that. Pity and compassion were words that devalued her feeling for Vellai. If her heart leapt with a desire to take him in her arms as soon as he appeared, could that feeling be called just pity?

'So what if he sees you, Vellai? It is not as if he hates you.'

'He will yell at me.'

'He won't. Come near me. Sit down.'

He sat in front of the house.

'Come in, Vellai.'

'No, I will sit here itself.'

Was he only seven years old? No, he was hundreds of years old and this response was rooted in the cumulative age of centuries. She must be patient.

'Here, payasam.'

'But this is your bowl...'

'I know...just drink.'

The centuries-old hands that accepted the bowl poured the payasam into the mouth of a seven-year-old who relished the sweetness.

She had heard that a nomadic group had brought Vellai to the kuppam when he was two years old. She knew his caste, and that his parents had succumbed to cholera. No other detail was known except one, which only Tulasi knew – that she melted when she saw him.

'Tastes good?' She stroked his head, but he moved away.

'Don't touch me, please.'

'I don't feel any electric shock…'

He smiled. An unspoken gratitude flashed quietly across that dark face.

'I asked you if it tastes good.'

'It is very nice, Amma…'

Amma…a term of respect. Was that all? The yearning in his eyes and the expression that filled them…was it just that?

The mere word 'Amma', commonly used with respect and sometimes indulgence, would not assuage her need. When it was used to address her, it should carry with it the very essence of life, as if it were the transcendental Om. Only then would her need be fulfilled, bringing with it a glow of satisfaction.

'If you have a deeply felt need like that, nothing wrong, Tulasi. Every girl is a mother. But why can't you adopt a suitable child from any of the good adoption centres?' This was Appa.

Appa did not understand. If she had felt the need first, she would have made arrangements to fulfil that need. But for her the fulfilment had come first and it was later she realized that she had a need. Until she saw Vellai, she, who had become a young woman, then a wife and then a childless widow, had not known that she had actually become a mother. It was only when he first appeared before her that she felt she had been waiting just for him all this time. The son appeared and transformed her into a mother. What was the sense in asking her to adopt some other child?

'Even before you were born, my darling, you were in the dreams of my womanhood, and in my girlish games!' She remembered some such lines written by Gurudev Tagore on a mother speaking to a child. The pure truth of that emotion! Had she been like that too, bearing Vellai in her heart, her life, her breath, her thoughts and her dreams, as her ideal right from the moment she was born?

When she was a child, Srinivasan was in Trichy, working as the assistant priest in a temple. As he would emerge from his bath, 'ritually pure' to perform his duties, she would fall on him playfully, and he would gently chide her.

Had Vellai been there in that joy which throbbed within her as she laughed then?

Had Vellai been in the rising wonderment as she sat next to the driver's seat in the town bus, turning her child's eyes this way and that, as the streets, houses, trees and people raced past?

Had Vellai been in the suffocating beauty of the distant sight of gods Ganesha and Ranganatha on either side of the road?

Had Vellai been in the thrill that shivered through her as she thought of the devotion of Tiruppaanazhvar,[5] who, having seen the nectar that was Ranganatha's beauty, wanted nothing more?

They used to live on Mela Chintamani. The Kaveri flowed behind the row of houses. When the river was swollen with water, Tulasi could just open the back door and step down to romp in and play with the Kaveri. It was on one such afternoon, as she was sitting on the steps down the river bank, splashing her feet in the water, when her father informed her that her marriage had been fixed.

Had Vellai been the source of the joy that stirred in her very being then?

'Shall I wash the tumbler and put it in the backyard?' Vellai had finished drinking the payasam.

'No need. Give it to me.' Tulasi smiled at him. 'Hey Vellai, do you like me?'

The boy looked up, the speechless lips trembled and tears filled his eyes. The next moment, Tulasi took him into her arms. He did not move away this time. That embrace transcended all objections.

'Amma…Amma.'

She said nothing and continued to hold him in her arms.

Her married life was happy, but short. After that tragic blow, Srinivasan did not want to stay there and moved to Madras. Tulasi started managing the house after her mother died.

Her father felt a sense of despair when he saw his daughter, who smiled on the outside but was desolate at heart. He wished desperately that she had had a child, for then, this emptiness would have been filled.

It was then she informed him that she had a seven-year-old son. Srinivasan was shocked. If she wanted a child, she could very well adopt a child from a 'good' place. Was he the only child available? What would the world say? Think of Srinivasan's caste and lineage, and his daughter goes and adopts a…thoooo! The thought nauseated even him. Tulasi was affectionate towards all the children around and, in the beginning, he thought Vellai was just one of them. He had not imagined that it would grow so deep. From whichever angle he viewed it, all he felt was confounded.

Will Tulasi never change her mind?

Shall I say yes to my only child's only wish?

Che che…that panchama boy as a grandchild.

Narayana…Could I ever wash off that sin?

But Tulasi is yearning for him. And that little one, with his single 'Amma' evokes an eternal link and tugs at her heart.

What shall I do?

Only my Narayana should guide me.

At this thought, his heart would grow lighter. He would commence his daily rituals with the relief of one who has shifted the weight from his shoulders on to those of another. Srinivasan entered the temple and felt rejuvenated at once. As he began his daily rituals, all other thoughts and worries were forgotten.

There wasn't a big crowd at the temple. One of the devotees broke a coconut as his prayers had been answered. Another paid for a feast at which sakkarai pongal would be offered to the deity on the occasion of the second birthday of his child. Another regular devotee arranged for the tirumanjanam.

211

Srinivasan began the tirumanjanam for the moolavar. The idol stood with just a cloth wrapped around the middle. He gently massaged it with oil, as one would do to a living being. Next, he poured water on it, followed by milk, curds and coconut water. He poured water again. Then the fragrant sambirani and the ritual prayer. The doors of the sanctum were closed. When they opened again, the deity was covered with sandal paste. Again the prayer and the pouring of water. Simultaneously, another priest was performing the same rituals to the urchava idol. The boy who rang the temple bell kept bringing them the water in copper vessels.

There was a feeling of complete surrender in Srinivasan's heart as he performed all these rituals with devotion and meticulous care.

'Narayana, you must show the way. I surrender to you.'

When the doors shut for the second time, a child in the crowd insisted loudly that he should go in too. The father took him away to distract him.

When the doors opened again, the freshly bathed idol stood resplendent in a new costume, shining jewels, silver disc, conch and fragrant garlands. The ritual prayers were performed to the clanging of the bell. The devotees offered their respects with devotion and amazement.

The tirumanjana materials were distributed to the devotees by Srinivasan. When he returned home after finishing all his duties, it was one. The food served by Tulasi energized him.

'Appa, just lie down and rest.'

'I will.'

'Your face looks very tired.'

'I am getting old, Amma. So I get exhausted.'

He lay down on the floor with his head on a block of wood. For a while, he just lay there listening to the sounds made by the vendor of stainless steel vessels, and the unseen birds which tweeted from inside tree holes, and then he dozed off. He felt refreshed when he woke up after a while.

'Will you come to the temple in the evening, Tulasi?'

'Mmm.'

'You say yes, but you will not come.'

'If you invite me and then say this, what do I do?' Tulasi laughed.

'I have been noticing what you do, and that is why I said so. How many times have I called you? I feel you might get some peace if you come. You say yes, but you never do. If you come once in ten times, it is too much.'

'It just does not happen.'

'You don't want to. Say that.'

'Why would I not want to, Appa?'

'You are angry with god.'

'Nothing of that sort.'

'When you were a child, your head would burst if you didn't visit the Ganesha temple every other day. If we went to Srirangam temple, you would refuse to come away.'

'That was when I was a child. Now I realize that devotion does not mean merely going to the temple. Does that mean I have no faith?'

'Then you come this evening. Or any evening or morning.'

213

'I'll come in the evening. Not in the morning.'

'Why? Because that brat will come in the morning?' He looked at her with piercing eyes.

Tulasi did not speak.

'Isn't that the reason, Tulasi?'

'Not just that, Appa. You may do the tirumanjanam in the morning.'

'So what?'

'I detest that ritual.'

'Why?'

'We bathing the god? Meaningless.'

'That is just a manifestation of our love, our devotion. In every act, we offer god our heart. Isn't it a symbol of our closeness that we tie a cloth around his middle, massage him with oil, bathe him, and then light the sambirani so that he does not catch a cold…'

'Rubbish. Will god catch a cold like us mortals?'

'Didn't I tell you? It is a symbol, a beautiful manifestation of our love, closeness…'

'That is what you say. You know what I think? By performing these rituals, we display our infantile behaviour. Bathing god like bathing mortals and lighting the sambirani to prevent a cold…Cold!' She burst out laughing. She stopped and asked with a measured dignity, 'Why, Appa, if we believe in an omnipresence that is god, should we see ourselves in that god? Isn't it greater to see that god in ourselves?'

He felt as if someone had shaken his very being. He looked at his daughter's face as one would stare with wonder, shock and fear at the sudden glow of knowledge emanating from a guru's words.

Narayana ... is this your voice, your words, your reply?

If we saw divinity in ourselves, if we saw divinity in all of us, then what was the meaning of these differences?

'Tulasi.' His voice and his body shook.

'Appa, I spoke out of turn. There is no sastra that you do not know. Who am I to advise you? What do I know? Forgive me ...'

'What do *you* know? ... What do *you* know?' His voice was unsteady and his heart restless.

'All that I know is ...'

'Tell me ... Amma ...'

'I only know I want that child.'

He trembled and his eyes wavered, and then fixed themselves on the wall. It was the picture that Tulasi had hung there of a toothless, grinning old man. Was he just the father of our nation? Didn't he teach us 'not untouchables, but Harijans'? Hari's children. As Tulasi said, that Mahatma had seen god in every human being. He was not an ideal hero who had lived in some grey historic past or resided in imagined dwellings; he had lived amongst us, just now, with us, and had lived what he believed.

Time passed unnoticed. He sat with his head bowed down. Tulasi rose and lit the lamp.

'Isn't it time to go to the temple?'

He saw an exaggerated smile on her face, meant to hide that she had washed her face to remove the traces of tears. He looked at her once. He was in turmoil.

There was a sound of rushing feet and two young men from the neighbourhood entered.

'Sir, did you see the paper? What a horror!' One of them, his face red, brandished a newspaper.

'What happened?'

'This news. It seems two Harijan boys have been burnt alive because of some dispute.'

He went on to describe in detail what happened and where, and when and why. Srinivasan stood there staring without comprehending anything.

What unspeakable cruelty! Whatever the provocation, how could one do this? Was it because they were Harijans? Whatever the differences between man and man, could discrimination scale such heights? He could not even imagine it. His blood boiled.

The next moment, he was calm. There was no confusion.

Was god making him aware of the inhumanly deep marks caused by the fetters that had tied us down for centuries? Was god saying it was horrible to drive Him away from his heart and installing the demon there?

'Isn't it greater to see god in ourselves?' That was only Narayana speaking.

'These differences should disappear. They must disappear. Every one of us must remove the differences at their level. Only then will they be rooted out.' Srinivasan declared, as if he was possessed. Then he turned to his daughter who was taken by surprise.

'True, Tulasi. God does not need tirumanjanam. It's we who need a cleansing, to remove the grime and attain divinity and purity.'

Tulasi stood in amazement. Then she understood his words and her body thrilled all over. She felt a dark figure snuggling next to her like a calf, whispering 'Amma'.

eighteen

Beneath the Ashes

THE LIVES OF SOME PEOPLE make you wonder if the words 'life' and 'death' have any meaning. They are born and go through life just breathing, till one day death comes. In that short span, some experience happiness, others sadness. Both kinds are linear and common – insipid, without any exciting moments or actions; mere heaps of ash without any glow.

Was there any meaning in Rajamani Maami's life?

Rajamani. The motherless child of a poor cook in a Vishnu temple, married at eighteen to a clerk in a private company, gave birth to a son at nineteen and lost him when she was nineteen-and-a-half. At twenty-one, she was a weak invalid after two miscarriages, and when she was twenty-one years and three months old, she was a 'vazhavetti' – her husband had deserted her.[3]

Even now at fifty-one, she was a vazhavetti as she lay dead in front of me.

Brahma the creator must have been in a happy mood when he sat down to create Rajamani. As he began his job from the feet, he must have focused on fashioning a body that was beauty at its peak. Skin the colour of burnished gold, graceful feet, slender fingers, slim and graceful legs, sculpted waist, breasts and neck…then…then what happened to Brahma? Why did his hands falter? He must have been thinking of the verse which says that Brahma's creations are destructible, but the creations blessed by his wife Saraswathi, the goddess of learning, are immortal. Consumed by envy of his wife, his attention must have strayed. And a scarecrow's head got fixed on Venus' body.

The private company's clerk must have seen her body when he saw her and nodded his head.

The poor father must have deemed himself fortunate that there was no demand for dowry. Rajamani got married. She wondered at her own good fortune. That clerk was no Manmatha – god of love. But next to her, any man would seem like a hundred Manmathas.

The husband became aware of her face only in her twenty-first year. It was as if he saw the protruding teeth, flattened nose, bulging eyes and wispy hair for the first time. He flinched. He found someone else very soon and deserted her.

It took her three years to figure out that he would not return to her. She went back to her father's house, a vazhavetti, and inherited his 'cook's ladle'. She made food for her husband and waited for him to return to her. How could she let him go unfed if he decided to return to her? When she had her periods, her employers would not let her cook, as according to the customs, she was 'unclean'. Even her father would not eat the food touched by her. He would not let her eat the temple food either. He would cook for her at home. She would reserve half of it for the husband who may return.

For three years, Rajamani waited with food every day, ready to serve her husband. One thousand…ninety-five…days.

Then one morning, she ate all the food that her father had cooked.

'What is this, Raji?'

She scooped up all the rice left in the bowl by her father, heaped it on the leaf, and poured the butter milk and all the vatha kuzhambu on it. She had two mouthfuls with relish, looked up and smiled.

The bulging eyes were blank.

Her body, which had become emaciated after one delivery, two miscarriages and three years of anxious waiting, slowly started to gain weight.

It was then that the penniless cook had a stroke and was paralysed.

Rajamani took the responsibility of taking care of her father. She offered to cook at the temple in her father's stead. The priest was a good man. He agreed. He engaged a substitute cook for 'those three days'. He treated her with dignity, as if she was his own daughter. But soon people began to gossip.

'What shall I do? God is our witness, our hearts are faultless. I'm aged and you are young. I know your troubles.

Please don't think I am condemning you to starvation. But a temple priest must be above suspicion...' His eyes were wet.

She looked at him silently for a few minutes, then fell at his feet. She left the place. She and her father had to eat; the invalid had to receive treatment and care. The income from the temple had covered these needs. She had given up working as a domestic helper in some houses, relying instead on the temple income. In any case, she did not have the time to take up such jobs, as she had to attend to her father.

Now when she went back to those houses, she found that others had replaced her.

She started hunting for jobs in earnest. She found two jobs eight kilometres away.

Rain or shine, she woke up at three, bathed her father, made him do some light exercises, gave him coffee, drank something herself, cooked some rice, took a bath and humbly requested the elderly lady in the next portion to take care of her father. Before her 'see you, Appa' faded out of earshot, she would be at the bus stop, by six. If on the odd day she was late by even ten minutes, she would be treated to a stiff lecture.

'You must come at the agreed time, otherwise you must stay at home in luxury, like a queen!'

The worry, the exertion and the work wore her out, but the expenses and debts kept going up.

When she was twenty-eight, her father died.

No doubt she had to spend less now, but the sorrow in her heart grew heavier. Even though he had been an invalid who lay curled up in a corner, the thought that he was there used to give her strength. Now she was totally alone. An unaccompanied vazhavetti was seen as fair game by men, and this had to be tackled.

'Rajimma,' he would call her. 'Narayana,' he would moan in pain. Now that he was gone, all she had was her yearning to hear his voice again.

The relentless work during all seasons took a toll on her health. She caught pneumonia and was bedridden for three weeks. Kind neighbours helped, but the debt burden grew heavier. Debt of gratitude, financial debt…No one demanded repayment. They said, 'The needy have to help the needy.' Gratitude flowed from her eyes. Her body had lost half its strength by the time she recovered, but it had not lost its beauty.

'How can you take leave without telling us?…How can we know…did you tell us? You may leave.' The doors of the places where she worked closed to her.

Without any work, hunger gnawed at her. The neighbours were not millionaires. They, too, led a hand-to-mouth existence. They helped when there was a crisis, but they could not support her on a daily basis.

The owner of her two-room portion offered to help. He said he would take care of her and that she need not work. He even offered to waive the rent arrears. But he demanded a price for that.

She was not willing.

She gave him her golden earrings, her only asset, which her father had bought for her when gold was not so dear. She asked him to adjust her dues against her earrings.

'So you intend to continue here rent-free? Just get out.'

She got out.

She stayed with a family known to the temple priest and searched for work. She found a job as an attendant in a private hospital. The work she had to do there day and night broke her back. At a moment's notice, she had to play the roles of an attendant, nurse, bathroom cleaner, cook and more. She did it until she was thirty-five.

One day when she was cleaning the toilet, she coughed. She thought it was the acrid smell of the disinfectant. She coughed again. This time she saw blood.

Could there be a better place for a sick person than a hospital? But tuberculosis is infectious. The male doctors touched her and examined her, they felt her chest with stethoscopes again and again, had X-rays taken while she stood with just a small towel around her and finally confirmed that it was indeed tuberculosis. How could she continue working there after that? Should they not think of her co-workers and the patients? The management said, 'Poor Rajamani. Good worker. What a pity.' The management gave her medicines for a month, salary for a month and sent her off.

Four months later, a member of a women's service organization found her lying on the road in the hot sun, unconscious with hunger and tuberculosis. She took her to their centre, a brick and mortar building which was the epitome of compassion and humanity. Rajamani found shelter there, and received treatment too.

223

After she was cured, she remained there doing whatever odd jobs she could. They taught the destitute women life skills to make them self-reliant. She learnt tailoring and bag-making. The income she earned was returned to the centre. She helped in the kitchen too.

The women at the centre were not bound to remain there. They could leave if they found a job that helped them live with dignity.

The lady who headed the centre was known to my aunt's friend. My aunt's live-in cook, who had worked for her for a long time, had died and she was on the look-out for another. So her friend approached the centre.

'Decent family, good people…They want a good woman cook. They will pay fair wages. Is there anyone at the centre?'

This is how Rajamani came to work for my aunt. I went to see my aunt a few days after that. Rajamani came in with the coffee and I was stunned by her figure. This in spite of the fact that she was forty-two then and I was only twenty, doing my postgraduate studies.

I quickly turned away, as it was indecent to stare like that. The protruding teeth, flattened nose, bulging eyes and wispy hair were quite repulsive.

Rajamani Maami worked in my aunt's house for nine years. After they became close, she shared the story of her life with my aunt. My aunt shared it with me. One day, while working, a spark of fire hurt her right eye. In spite of treatment, that eye lost its vision. Though my aunt offered to help her, Maami refused outright. She cooked food fit for the gods with that single eye. One Sunday afternoon, she served that wonderful food to everyone at home and went to bed with a headache. She fell unconscious and was admitted in a government hospital. After two weeks, she died. It was a brain tumour.

My aunt, her eyes red and swollen with tears, asked me to light the pyre. Her son was a professor in Germany. Had he been here, she would have asked him to do it.

I agreed.

I stood in the Otteri cremation ground, looking at Maami for the last time, looking at Maami on the funeral pyre. At twenty-nine I now had the maturity to think of Rajamani Maami the person, transcending the lovely body and the unlovely face. Was there a meaning to her life? A dull life and a dull death. Was this life? She had lived through a chain of miseries, relentless misfortune…a good soul tormented by fate…a woman to be pitied.

I lit the fire.

My aunt had turned back and walked some distance.

I stood looking at the flames for a while and then turned. Behind me stood a man of medium height, with grey hair and a wrinkled face, wearing a bright polyester shirt and veshti. His eyes were still wet.

As I turned, he raised his hands in a namaskaram to me and started to go away.

I was intrigued.

'Sir, please wait.'

He waited.

'I don't know you. Why did you greet me like that?'

'My gratitude for lighting her pyre,' he said in a low voice, after a moment's pause.

He had used the singular pronoun, so he must be an acquaintance. Otherwise he would not be disrespectful.

'Sorry, but how are you related to Maami?'

'Her husband.'

After the first frozen moments, my contempt burst out.

'Oh! You are the husband who abandoned the girl at twenty, making her a vazhavetti.'

'Raji need not have been that all her life. A few years after I left her, I repented and cut off all my undesirable connections and searched for her. I had resigned from my post as a clerk and had started a hardware business, and I was doing well then. She was thirty then. Her father had died, she was on the streets looking for a job. I sought her forgiveness and asked her to return to me. She refused.'

'An insipid life,' we thought, but from the heap of ashes had risen a glowing spark.

I cannot decide if what Maami did was right or wrong. I do not have an answer to the moral question of whether a repentant man should be denied pardon. Nor could I fathom the feelings of a woman who waited with cooked food for one thousand and ninety-five days, only to be disappointed.

But something must have happened. Her self-respect must have been deeply wounded. Sorrow may have hardened into resignation. Love may have died forever. Whatever the reason, when the moment came for her to choose between joy and misery, she chose the latter. She could have put an end to all her troubles by agreeing to live with her husband in comfort. That was the moment of truth in her life. And she chose to do what she thought was right. The life of drudgery that she chose was not one to be pitied. It was a life that deserved respect. It was a life of dignity.

That dignity must have been her secret treasure. When she poured out the details of her life to my aunt, why did she not tell her about this meeting with her husband?

I really saw Rajamani Maami only after she died.

When did that man leave?

I walked up to my aunt.

'Poor Rajamani!' she sighed.

I said nothing.

Acknowledgements

This is my second book of translations and I would like to thank a few people who I will name in a random order.

Brian Harris is a pioneering figure in translation, among the first to put forward several ideas such as translator's affinity, with the most important of his ideas being 'natural translation', especially by children. He took the trouble to write to me from Valencia when he read my translation of Seetha Ravi's short stories in *The Hindu* online. I thank him for the lovely friendship that was born thereafter and for what I have learnt about translation from him.

I thank my grand aunt, K. Savitri Ammal – whose translation of Rt Hon'ble Srinivasa Sastri's *Lectures on Ramayana* into Tamizh reads like an original – for passing on her genes.

Vatsala, the Tamizh poet, was the first person to read the stories in this book and she did the first editing. I thank her for devoting her time to this venture so generously and cheerfully. I thank Ms Chandana and Medha for contributing to the editing. I thank Ms Netra Shyam for designing the cover. I am grateful to Ratna Books for asking me to take up this work and for doing such a good job of bringing out the book.

I thank Ambai for writing about her dear friend on the back cover; it has added value. I also thank Professor K. Bharathi of the R. Chudamani Memorial Trust for making this book possible. I am grateful to the Madras Players and Mr P.C. Ramakrishna for the play *Chudamani*, based on my translation of her short stories, including three from this collection. The continuing success of the play tells me that Chudamani the writer is as fresh as ever – to whom I owe a great deal of gratitude.

PRABHA SRIDEVAN

Notes

1. (p. 20): The azhvars were Vaishnavite saints. The first three were Peyazhvar, Boothathazhvar and Poigaiyazhvar. The story goes that on a rainy night, one of them took shelter under a roof and lay down. The second came and asked the first if there was room for him. The first azhvar said there was room for two to sit. Next, the third azhvar came and was told that there was room for three to stand. Then they felt another presence crowding them out – this was Vishnu.

2. (p. 83): Seetha's wedding (Parinayam) with Rama, the coronation of Rama's sandals (Paduka Pattabhishekam) by his brother Bharatha, and Rama's coronation (Pattabhishekam) are the three episodes considered to be very auspicious in the Ramayana.

3. (pp. 106, 218ff): 'Vazhavetti' refers to a woman deserted by her husband. It could literally be 'the one with a wasted life'. Since the word carries a stigma, many women remain in an abusive marital home.

4. (p. 194): Tyagaraja, also named Tyagabrahmam, was a music composer and saint. Along with Muthuswami Dikshitar and Syama Sastri, he forms the musical trinity of south Indian classical music.

5. (p. 209): Twelve persons – the azhvars – are revered as the prime devotees by Vaishnavites. One of them is Tiruppanazhvar, who by birth belonged to a caste which was considered untouchable.